The Rose & the Ring
Book Two

Lady Katherine

Joyce Williams

DEDICATION

To my forever friend Sherrill, who continually

encourages me to keep writing.

Cover art: *Ophelia* by John Waterhouse

Copyright © 2014 Joyce Williams

ISBN-10: 1503386384
ISBN-13: 978-1503386389

RECOGNITION:

To Devorah Nelson, www.storydoctor.blogspot.com,

for her help with character development, story

structure and editing; and to Aimee Stewart,

www.foxfires.com, for creating the cover art for *The

Rose & The Ring* series using public domain paintings

by John Waterhouse. I am indeed grateful!

AUTHOR'S NOTE

The inspiration for this book came in 1993 during our first trip to the Czech Republic, only recently freed from communism. We flew into Prague and then rode nine hours to Pordubice, the city where our friends lived. On nearly every high hill looking down on the countryside below, there stood a castle. Some had become tourist attractions while others crumbled in ruins. By the time we arrived at our destination, my curiosity was in full swing.

On a free day, our husbands asked my friend and me what we would like to do. "Visit a castle!" was our immediate response. Four pairs of eyes got big and four wiggly bodies got wigglier still as the couple's four children jumped up and down, begging, "Can we? Oh, can we, please!?"

Our friends lived in a three-room dormitory suite. They had no personal transportation. They ate in a communal dining room—lots of cabbage soup and oatmeal—and very few people spoke English. So an adventure was definitely in order!

Bundling up against the October chill, we made our way to a local castle in a borrowed vehicle, got in line behind a busload of German tourists, and were waved on in after we donned one-size-fits-all house-slippers to protect the castle floors. The guide did not speak English, and we did not speak German or Czech. But the walls—oh, they spoke! This is their story.

"A kiss,

when all is said, what is it?

. . . a rosy dot placed on the "i" in loving;

'tis a secret told to the mouth

instead of to the ear."

--Edmond Rostand

December, 1439. Burg Mosel, Pomerania.

CHAPTER ONE

"You leave me alone, Nicklaus Branden." Ten-year-old Kitty O'Donnell's slender body quivered with indignation, and the bronze freckles dancing across her pert little nose itched to dart off and sting the rogue. Aiming a swift kick of her slim foot toward Nick's shins to emphasize her protest, Kitty declared war on the twelve-year-old boy who took great delight in teasing her with a ribbiting, bulging-eyed frog.

"But you're so funny when you're mad." Nick's impudent grin sealed his doom; Kitty's foot connected with his leg—and the frog made a wild leap to freedom.

"Ouch!" Nick yelped, hopping on one foot and rubbing his shin. "You kicked me!"

Kitty planted her fists at her waist with her elbows jutting out at right angles. Her eyes spit green fire. "Yes, I did. And I'm going to call you Naughty Nick."

Rolling his eyes, Nick taunted, "Ha! You can just call me *my lord*." After all, as master of a vast estate, his father held the title of Lord Branden—and Nick was the only heir.

"Never." Her flaming red curls bounced around her shoulders as she stomped off.

Kitty chuckled out loud; the old memory still evoked the childish satisfaction she'd felt at kicking Nick. But oh, how her feelings had changed!

She ran a slender hand over the marble-topped altar in Burg Mosel's Chapel of the Shepherd and whisked a few wayward pine needles off its gleaming surface. The in-house sanctuary, silent witness to every significant event in the lives of the ancestral residence's inhabitants, would soon mark Nick's return from Charles University in Prague. A letter addressed to his parents, Lord Erik and Lady Rosamund Branden, had arrived last week, announcing he would be home for Christmas.

Kitty glanced around the festively decorated chapel and let her eyes rest on the candles in the wrought iron advent wreath hanging by chains from the first of the half-dozen arches shouldering the frescoed ceiling. Three candles had already been lit, marking the traditional December Sunday advent meditations observed in accordance with the traditional Church calendar.

She tunneled her fingers through her coppery hair and pushed it back from her forehead. Steadying her excitement with a deep breath, Kitty hurried along the center aisle toward the doors opening into the corridor that connected the foyer with the tower. The jewel-toned sunlight slanting through the stained glass window warmed her back as she trailed her fingers over the arms of the simple wooden pews facing knee-worn prie-dieux.

Upon reaching the vaulted foyer, she started up the sweeping central staircase, pausing near the top to look back down over her shoulder at the massive oak doors with their wide iron bracings. Any day now, Nick would open those doors and walk back into her life.

Kitty smiled at the thought and bent to sniff the pine garland wrapped around the banisters. As she straightened, her gaze leveled with the mistletoe suspended from the entry hall's massive crystal chandelier—an unspoken invitation for a kiss. Oh, if only Nick would . . . She dragged her thoughts away from her cherished daydream and climbed the remaining steps.

Halting at the second doorway in the east wing corridor, Kitty's firm push opened the door. Despite a thorough cleaning and fresh pine boughs, Nick's chambers felt lived-in, as if he'd spring out from behind the dressing screen at any moment.

She could picture him dressed in riding clothes, hear him shouting, "Death to the Black Knight!" while he flexed his bone-handled leather whip. Not that he'd ever used it on a horse, but he'd certainly taken immense pleasure in cracking it in the air.

Her chuckle became a dry sob. One horse had deserved a good lashing. A black stallion named Thunder had thrown her father, Curtis O'Donnell, causing fatal head injuries. And when her mother had died a year later, Kitty's welfare—along with her self-confidence—fell to the charity of the Brandens.

Shaking her head to escape her heavy thoughts, Kitty backed out of Nick's doorway and headed to her own suite of rooms at the end of the passageway, rooms that had belonged to Lady Rosamund when she was a girl. Kitty crossed to the washstand that stood below the window, poured water from the porcelain ewer into a matching bowl, and rinsed her face and hands.

As she picked up the dainty linen towel, movement outside the window on the snow-covered drive caught her eye. A horse-drawn sleigh glided to a stop beside the broad marble steps that led to the front entrance. Her heart skipped a beat and her face flushed. The towel slipped unnoticed through her fingers.

Nick was home!

Sliding still-damp hands down the front panel of her dark green wool *cotte*, a structured over-dress, she rushed into the corridor and hurried toward the staircase. She heard the massive front doors groan as they opened, and by the time she reached the balustrade that skirted the balcony, two young men stood waiting in the foyer below.

One man had his back to her. His *ushanka*, a fur hat with ear flaps, covered his head and hid his face from her, but his shoulders appeared much too broad to be Nick's; she quickly dismissed him as a stranger.

The second man turned toward her, offering a

good look at his narrow, pale face. She didn't recognize him either.

Bewildered, Kitty retreated. Who were these men? Why were they here? Please, dear God, surely they did not bring bad news. She leaned against the mahogany-paneled wall and closed her eyes, her joyful anticipation dripping from her soul like melted candle wax.

In the next moment, staccato footsteps rushing toward the foyer snagged her attention. Her curiosity surmounting her disappointment, she straightened up and edged toward the railing.

"Mother!" the broad-shouldered man cried as he crushed Lady Branden in an exuberant hug, lifting her off her feet and whirling her around and around.

Kitty smothered her gasp with her hand. While she'd been leaning against the wall, both men had removed their *ushankas*, and she could now see that the tall, broad-shouldered stranger was indeed Nick—a mature Nick.

He eased his mother to her feet and came to a stop with the sunlight from the foyer's soaring vaulted window illuminating his face.

From her unseen vantage point, Kitty noted that

he looked every bit the aristocratic gentleman in his mink-trimmed gray wool cloak. Strength and purpose characterized his forehead, nose, and jaw. The slight cleft denting his square chin hinted at the general good humor behind his handsome face, and his smiling lips set her heart to hammering in her chest.

Lady Branden's unsteady whisper interrupted Kitty's perusal. "It's so good to have you home." A tremulous smile wreathed Nick's mother's face as she dashed away her happy tears with shaking fingers. When Nick chuckled and hugged her close one more time, Kitty's eyes prickled with unshed tears.

As Nick released his mother, he turned and reached out a hand to indicate the slender man waiting in the shadows. "This is Jacques Monet. I overheard him inquiring at the Red Deer Inn about potential lodging in one of the villages near here. I took one look at him and knew he wouldn't find anything suitable in the area, so I offered him the hospitality of Burg Mosel." He turned his head and completed the introduction. "My mother, Lady Branden."

The cut of Jacques's brown wool cloak bespoke a successful merchant, and Lady Branden's gracious reception held the deference appropriate to his station in life. "You are most welcome."

As Jacques acknowledged her greeting with a polite bow, Josef entered the foyer, toting Jacques's trunk.

Lady Branden turned and directed the servant in a low voice, "The green room, Josef."

Returning her attention to her son's guest, she invited, "Come, I'll show you to your room."

Filled with an inexplicable surge of anxiety over greeting this manly Nick and his cosmopolitan friend, Kitty shrank back in frantic haste. She clutched the skirt of her *cotte* with both hands and sped silently toward the door to her chambers.

But the blush that burned her cheeks could not be solely credited to her sudden exertion. After all, she had secretly loved Nick for almost as long as she could remember, though nobody, she felt sure, suspected it. Least of all, Nick.

* * *

"When did you leave Prague, Nicky?" Jacques lifted an eyebrow and smirked when his hostess used her son's boyhood nickname.

"Eight days ago today," Nick replied. "I would

have arrived home sooner, but I got caught in a snow storm and ended up staying two days in a small hut with a farmer and his wife, their six children, their chickens, and a goat. Last night, I finally got a decent meal and a hot bath at the Red Deer Inn. I was glad not to arrive here in my former state. You wouldn't have let me through the front gate, Mother," he teased.

Lady Branden put out her fingers and touched his hand in silent reassurance that nothing so trivial could have spoiled her welcome. Nick wrapped her fingers in his. As their eyes met, a happy glow bathed her face.

Trailing several steps behind mother and son, Jacques observed this intimate communication. He grimaced and twisted his lips into a smile when Josef started down the stairs toward them.

Nick pushed open the door to the guest room and then stood aside for his mother and Jacques to enter.

Lady Branden crossed the navy, green, and ivory wool rug that covered most of the polished wood floor. She gave the window latch a sharp twist, opening the shutters. Sunlight streamed through the glass; it fingered the navy velvet curtains that enclosed the bed and reflected off the brass fireplace screen that reminded him of peacock feathers spread in full courtship display.

"I hope you'll be comfortable here." Lady Branden's warm smile emphasized the sincerity of her welcome. "The dinner bell will announce meals. Give the bell cord a tug if you need anything; a servant will come at your call." She motioned toward the tasseled bell pull near the fireplace. "And after you're settled, feel free to come downstairs and relax in the great room at the end of the corridor directly below us."

As soon as they were gone, Jacques removed his cloak and tossed it and his *ushanka* on the bed. He spun around and strode to the window, where he stared down at the snow-covered drive. As he lifted his eyes to the surrounding stone wall, he visualized the snow-frosted countryside beyond. Such richness. And noble-born Nick would inherit it all.

He recalled their conversation yesterday while they waited outside the Red Deer Inn for the sleigh Nick had hired to transport them to Burg Mosel. "A big ship must be turned slowly if the transition is to be smooth," Nick had remarked. Then, almost as an afterthought, he'd added, "My father told me that—he captained a Hansa cog before he married my mother."

"And what big ship do you mean to turn, Nick?" Jacques had hoped his lazy, half-amused manner belied his interest.

"My family estate, for a start. And that's where you come in. I'm going to look for an opportunity to encourage my father to invite the Hanseatic League to establish a connection in one of our villages—I think we could export local Bohemian *forest glass*, for a start. My father works hard to promote the villagers' welfare, but there's a lot more we can do. The present undercurrent of social unrest, particularly the peasant uprisings, tells me that change is inevitable. I want to work with that knowledge, not against it.

Walking every day through the Old Town Square in Prague and passing the places where the martyr, Jan Hus, lived, preached, and taught, helped me see that oppression and ignored frustration serves as a seed-bed for rebellion. I took a lesson from that tragedy. As landowners, we have a choice; we can make slow concessions that will work to our advantage over time or we can squelch reform and foster a revolution."

Jacques shook his head at the remembered conversation. Only a fool would give up the benefits enjoyed by those born with wealth or shrewd enough to acquire it. Dark determination crossed his face as he wheeled from the window and dropped on one knee beside his trunk.

His nimble fingers located and pressed the hidden spring to release the chest's false bottom. A secret drawer slid out, exposing a rectangular metal box. One glance assured him that his father's journal remained safe. He snapped the drawer shut and sank back on his heels. This was the moment he'd anticipated since his father's death twelve years ago.

The Brandens had caused his father's misfortune and his family's ensuing misery. Now, revenge was his mission. Patience would have its reward. And it would be sweet.

* * *

Nick halted in his boyhood room, welcomed by the woodsy scent of holiday greenery as he wrapped his arms around his mother in another big hug. His whisper near her ear ruffled her dark hair. "I'm so glad to be home." He pressed her head close against his broad chest, where the steady rhythm of his heartbeat reassured her of his love.

When Nick released her, Lady Branden blinked vigorously and cleared her throat. "Don't be long. Your father will be in soon for our evening meal, and he'll be impatient to see you." She rose on her toes and kissed his cheek before she departed.

His eyes alight with nostalgia, Nick moved farther into the room. Nothing had changed. He reached out and ran his long fingers over the bone handle of his leather riding crop that hung on the wall by the fireplace, a gift from Lord Nicklaus Schmidden, his grandfather and namesake. His gaze continued around the room and finally settled on the map of the night sky that covered much of one wall.

A warm reminiscence stirred his heart. His father, Lord Erik Branden, had told him it was the constellation chart he'd followed to keep him on course during his many expeditions running cargo for the Hanseatic League in his youth. And years later the chart had served as their guide when, together, they had explored the night sky.

Nick's gaze shifted to the window seat. The

familiar indentations in the large, tassel-trimmed blue cushions propped against the casement invited him to come and lean into them again like his custom in the past when he wanted to be alone with his thoughts. Why, even the pheasant feather quill pen Kitty had given him for his last birthday at home still stood in the empty ink well.

Kitty. He chuckled at the thought of her, recalling the day he'd teased her with a frog and she'd retaliated by kicking him.

CHAPTER TWO

Kitty perched on the edge of the padded stool and leaned her elbows on her marble-topped dressing table. She felt anxious. Why? She didn't exactly know. Could it be because the object of her hero worship was no longer far away and safe to idolize? Staring down at Nick from the balcony a few minutes earlier, she'd realized he was not the boy who'd gone away. He was a man.

She pushed aside her thoughts and leaped up to discard her everyday homespun. Slipping into her most becoming *cotte*, fashioned in saffron-colored silk, she secretly hoped its scooped neckline and shapely fit would awaken Nick to her maturing femininity.

She loosened the drawstrings of a small purple silk bag and tipped out the dainty string of pearls, her First Communion gift from her benefactors. With the strand resting against her throat, she bent her head and slipped the toggle into the ring at the back of her neck. Smoothing her fingers over the pearls, she pressed them lightly against her fair skin as she stole a hopeful glance at her reflection.

The gown hugged her curves in the bodice and sleeves and then eased into a long, draping skirt made especially graceful by inserted gores. The simple necklace added an elegant finishing touch.

Her small bottle of scented oil caught her attention. Grabbing it up, she laughed softly when the cork made its usual popping sound as she removed the stopper. A swift daub at her throat and another at each of her wrists enveloped her in the sweetly exotic aroma. The corners of her mouth tipped up; surely Nick would remember her familiar jasmine scent.

Kitty grinned back at her mirrored image and dropped a flirtatious curtsey. The nervous churning in her stomach, though unsettling, did not prove sufficient to shake her confidence that she looked her best. She pinched her cheeks until they stung with a rosy flush and admonished the girl in the mirror, "Lady Branden taught you how to behave like a lady. Now don't shame her." Twirling impulsively in a pirouette of excitement, she headed to the door, swung it open, and stepped into the hallway.

Behind her, at the end of the long corridor, smoldering rays of afternoon sunshine streaked through the high window. The wispy curls that tugged free from her mesh *crespine* trapped the sunlight in a copper halo around her face, and her pearls gleamed as they shifted against her bare skin. The silk threads in her gown shimmered luminously in the light.

Up ahead, Nick's door opened and he stepped into the corridor.

Seeing up close his fashionably cropped hair and stylish garments that reflected his sophistication and maturity, Kitty's mouth went dry and her trembling fingers pinched pleats in her skirt in nervous spasms.

Immediately, a taunting inner voice told her she had surely lived in a fool's paradise while Nick was away, secretly imagining that she'd captivate his imagination when he came home. Determined not to humiliate herself, she lifted her chin and closed the space between them.

But when blue eyes met green in a flash of mutual recognition, Kitty's emotions overruled her dignified intentions; she threw her arms around him and cried, "Nicky, you're home, you're home!"

* * *

Nick felt as if he'd suddenly plunged head-first into a blazing blacksmith's forge. Kitty! What a glorious creature of fire and light. As she hugged him in a burst of joy, his arms instinctively wrapped around her, pressing her close. With his head bent and his cheek resting on her flaming hair, the feel of her in his arms shook him to the root of his soul. Her familiar jasmine scent seared through his innate reserve, torching a latent flame.

In the next moment Nick impulsively pressed his lips to the top of Kitty's head, then near her ear, and on down to her cheek. Finally, his lips found hers. And after a tentative moment of surprise, what innocently began in wonder became a passionate kiss—a kiss as fiery as the sun's radiance engulfing them.

After what seemed a heart-stopping eternity, Kitty gasped for air, causing Nick to loosen his grip. She pulled back in the circle of his arms, but he felt reluctant to let her go. Still holding her, he drank in her glowing face, her shining curls, her feminine

figure. Their eyes met, speaking secrets not yet
formed into words.

"Ahem! I wish a lovely lady would welcome me
home with such enthusiasm."

Startled, Nick's arms dropped as he and Kitty
veered toward the voice that interrupted them.
Seeing Jacques at the top of the stairs, Nick's jaw
tightened as he struggled to regain his shaken
composure.

He motioned toward his guest, explaining, "Kitty,
this is Jacques Monet. I met him on my way home and
offered Burg Mosel's hospitality." He swallowed hard
to smooth his strained voice before he finished the
introduction. "Jacques, this is Kitty O'Donnell. Kitty is
my parents' ward. She's been like a sister to me."

Jacques acknowledged Kitty with a courteous
nod, but he muttered under his breath, "Quite a
sister."

* * *

Like a sister! Nick's words slashed through
Kitty's heart like a well-honed knife blade, and her
greeting got stuck in her throat.

"Ah . . . Nick and I are childhood friends . . . a-and
we haven't seen each other for three years." She

gulped for air and clasped her hands together so tightly that her nails cut into her palms. "We're all happy to have him home."

The atmosphere seemed to thicken. Nick refused to meet her gaze. And Jacques's raised eyebrows and narrowed eyes said he'd reached his own conclusion on how matters stood between them—no matter how vigorous her denial.

"Come, let's go downstairs. I'm anxious to see my father." Nick bolted to the staircase, pounding down the steps with his head bowed, not waiting to see if they followed.

When Jacques threw her a sympathetic glance before turning to follow Nick, Kitty's heart stung with humiliation. She stood frozen for several long moments before she lifted her skirts and slowly made her way down the stairs, ruthlessly scolding herself.

What happened to your resolve to behave graciously, the way Lady Branden trained you? What must Nick think of you, throwing yourself at him? No wonder he couldn't retreat fast enough; you embarrassed him in front of his guest. How can you ever face him again?

Shame rippled through her body, forcing her to

cling to the banister to prevent a tumble as she descended.

She headed along the east corridor and ducked into the dining hall, certain Jacques had followed Nick farther along the hallway to the great room. Her pulse throbbed wildly in her throat and her fair skin felt dry and hot. Desperate to collect her wits and recover her poise before she had to interact with them both at dinner, she collapsed on a carved-back chair and pressed her quivering fingers to her lips, lips which only moments before had been branded by Nick's kiss.

He *had* kissed her. No doubt about it.

And it wasn't a brother's kiss!

The very thought of the passion they'd shared sent a feverish heat surging through her body. She clapped her hands to her face and doubled over on an agonizing groan as her derisive inner voice berated her:

You hardly know each other after three years apart. You didn't even recognize him at first. And he just admitted he still thinks of you as his sister. Besides, he's the only son and heir of Lord and Lady Branden. And you—yes, you'd best face the cold, hard truth—

21

you're nothing but the orphaned daughter of an Irish clerk and a scullery maid, and furthermore, you are totally dependent on his parents' charity.

She'd always known the facts of her lowly status, but the Branden's generosity, her youthful adoration of Nick, and her foolish daydreams had obscured the reality of their social disparity. Now, gut-wrenching mortification swallowed up any remaining thrill at the memory of their kiss.

Since her mother's death, Lord and Lady Branden had treated her like a daughter, but it would be imprudent, indeed wickedly presumptuous, to expect any more from them. Nick was their pride and joy, their promise for the future. Surely, they intended him to make a brilliant marriage. One with political advantage. Comparable social status. Substantial property. His noble birth and outstanding education guaranteed him prestige among any class of people. And she must never forget her welcome in the Branden household depended on their compassion and favor. While her heart longed for Nick's love, daring to reach for it would certainly bring her heartache and disgrace.

But what could she do? Rash behavior would

dishonor the family she loved and who provided for her so generously. She knew her pampered life contrasted sharply with an unsupported woman's harsh existence. With no family of her own to fall back on, she couldn't afford to alienate the Brandens—or she just might end up in a convent for the rest of her life. If only she could marry someone respectable. A merchant, perhaps. Or an overseer for a wealthy landowner. Then maybe these feelings for Nick would go away.

Kitty straightened her shoulders, determined to suffocate all unruly thoughts. She would treat Nick like a brother. How else could she look him in the eyes? How else could she repay Lord and Lady Branden for their unfailing kindness?

CHAPTER THREE

Jacques followed Nick into the great room, his steps halting abruptly as he took in the impressive appointments. A jade statue on a round walnut table filled the center of the room. A massive tapestry dressed the wall above a long table featuring a pair of matching Chinese porcelain vases. Carved jade and white marble chess pieces on the gaming table in the corner stood in half-played-game positions.

A white-haired man sat in one of the two oversized chairs facing the fireplace. Nearby, a suit of armor, complete with pikestaff, reflected the fire's leaping flames. A small stool sat to one side of the hearth.

But it was the raven-haired young woman smiling down from the portrait mounted above the mantle that sucked the breath from Jacques's throat.

This was the portrait his father had written about in his journal; this was the woman his father had loved! With her delicate features and noble carriage, this lovely creature should have been his mother—not the work-worn harpy who'd been his father's late-in-life second choice.

"Greetings, Father." Nick's voice pulled Jacques back to the present.

The white-haired gentleman immediately stood to his feet. The crow's feet around his eyes were deep and he walked with a slight limp, but his smile held a boyish charm. He hugged his son and welcomed him with a hearty kiss on each cheek. As they gripped each other's arms their eyes met and held.

"Welcome home, Son."

"I'm very glad to be here," Nick said, his affection evident as he rested his arm across his father's shoulders and turned to introduce his guest. "Father, this is Jacques Monet. My father, Lord Branden."

The admiration that vibrated in Nick's voice caused a knot in Jacques's stomach and made him clench his fists behind his back. He choked down the jealous rage that rushed through his chest and pushed up to his lips. With concentrated effort he took himself to task; now that his destiny lay within his grasp, he simply could not allow his feelings to betray him.

The dinner bell rang before the three men could engage in further conversation. Lord Branden gestured with a wave of his hand for his son and his guest to precede him to the adjacent room.

Jacques observed that the dining hall at Burg Mosel was even more impressive than the great room. Gleaming mahogany paneling concealed the thick stone walls and provided an understated backdrop for several richly-hued Flemish tapestries. Shutters and dark blue watered silk draperies accented the recessed windows. Framed by elaborate moldings, the ceiling featured a central fresco of orange-throated blue swallows swooping among baby-faced cherubs floating on puffy white clouds.

The glow cast by the candles burning in the sixteen-arm chandelier mingled with the flickering firelight, and pale winter sunlight angled through the many small panes in the leaded glass windows that overlooked a snow-blanketed rose garden.

To the left of the fireplace, a matching pair of ornate-handled swords with crossed blades pointing upward formed a frame for a coat of arms, and even from a distance, Jacques could see that the heraldic charge featured a regardant red deer. He determined to question his host about the swords later.

As the men entered the room, Lady Branden turned from the gleaming refectory table laid with dinner service for five. Ecru lace defined the neckline of her ruby red *cotte* and trimmed the pointed ends of her bell-shaped sleeves. Centered on her forehead, a teardrop-shaped ruby was attached to a gold headband that circled her dark hair. Jacques was startled to recognize her strong resemblance to her mother, the woman in the painting in the great room.

He closed his eyes for a moment to center his mind on his vengeful goal—the only method he knew to control his rage. He forced his fists to relax; his purpose would not be served by losing his head, his heart, or his composure.

Lady Branden's soft, cultured voice summoned him from his bitter thoughts. "You may sit here, Jacques." She motioned to the black walnut side chair on Nick's right. The lion's head carved into the crest of its tall back matched the carvings on the remaining side chairs surrounding the table, and at a second glance he was almost certain they matched the two oversized chairs facing the fireplace in the great room. Someone had certainly taken great care with the details of gracious living.

Kitty, who had been standing at the window staring out at the rose garden, turned and joined them as everyone sat down.

When Lord Branden offered a dinner grace, the servants waited respectfully, but Jacques couldn't bring himself to close his eyes; the blessings the Brandens attributed to God would soon come to an end. That was precisely why he was here, sitting at this table with these, his avowed enemies.

As the servants placed the chargers holding trenchers filled with roasted venison, turnips, leeks, and carrots in front of the diners, Jacques noted that each attendant made a point to discreetly nod or wink at Nick. What would it be like, he wondered, to hold a special place in your servants' hearts?

Jealousy over Nick's welcome intensified Jacques struggle to maintain a pleasant expression on his face, so when Lord Branden interrupted his dark thoughts with an inquiry about his occupation, he paused to refocus.

"I—" he pressed his curled fist to his mouth and cleared his throat before starting again. "I work with the Hanseatic League, a confederation of merchants, trading guilds, and towns that have banded together to facilitate safe transport for goods exported along the major trade routes." He smoothed his thin fingers over his straight, sandy brown hair. "I began as an office boy, but now I'm the liaison between the League and five cities." He paused to temper his desire to boast. "My purpose for this trip is to establish new connections for the League."

Lord Branden's blue eyes brightened with interest and the laugh lines around his mouth and eyes deepened with his smile. "Well done, young man," he exclaimed, leaning forward. "I was a cargo runner for the Hansa in my youth." He chuckled. "That is, before I met and married my wife." He beamed at Lady Branden, obviously happy with his choice.

"Nick did mention that," Jacques commented, satisfied that downplaying his rise to a position of significance had been the right move.

Lord Branden continued, "I've considered encouraging the glass-blowers' guild in one of the larger villages along our eastern border with Bohemia to connect with the League, so your visit is providential. Meet me in my clerk's office tomorrow and we'll discuss this venture further." He turned to his son, "I'd be pleased if you'd join us, Nick."

"I'll be there." Nick nodded at his guest, adding, "Jacques and I already discussed this possibility."

Jacques's heart thudded with excitement, but he managed to keep his countenance steady. "I'd be honored to meet you, my lord. What time shall I be there?"

"Hmm . . . just after mid-day. That will give me ample time to finish other business. I want to give you my complete attention." He smiled warmly at their guest, and then concentrated on the sumptuous meal.

"What city are you from?" Breaking the silence, Kitty's husky contralto held only a polite effort at conversation.

She'd been so quiet that Jacques suspected she resented his presence diverting attention from Nick's long-awaited homecoming, and he secretly congratulated himself; anything that would drive her into Nick's arms would play out in his favor.

"I've always lived in Nuremberg," he answered her question and then deliberately continued with more information than she'd requested, "My father was a music teacher, but his sporadic work never provided an adequate living."

While he bent his lips in what passed as a smile, he gritted his teeth to restrain another sudden burst of anger, his instinctive response to his memories.

"He was forty-seven when he married my mother; she was his landlord's daughter. I was born one year later. I have two younger sisters who are both married and live in Nuremburg. My father apprenticed me to a cloth merchant when I was nine, with the stated hope that I would eventually achieve financial success. He died the winter I turned twelve. My mother died of consumption last year."

Jacques extended his left hand, displaying the small gold ring on his pinkie so each one seated around the table could see the two clasped hands that formed the ring's crown.

"My mother's. And her mother's before her." He didn't tell them that wearing his mother's ring kept his quest for revenge in front of his eyes and therefore at the forefront of his thoughts.

"It's a lovely keepsake." Lady Branden's comment made him stuff his hand back under the table, pretending sudden embarrassment.

"Now that my sisters are married, I'm on my own." He deliberately lowered his eyes to draw on the Brandens' sympathy while privately sneering at their gullibility.

"I expect they will want you home for Christmas, but you're certainly welcome to stay with us through the remainder of Advent. I've planned a musicale for Thursday evening. A traveling troupe as well as the young people from the neighboring estates have been invited to join us. You would make the group an even number. Do say you'll stay." His hostess's voice softened as she appealed to him.

"Oh, yes. Do stay." Kitty's enthusiasm surprised him. He fixed his eyes on her, and her ensuing blush filled him with elation.

"You'd be most welcome, young man." Lord Branden confirmed his wife's invitation. "Consider yourself part of our family during your stay, regardless of the business we transact tomorrow morning."

While Jacques chewed a bite of succulent

33

Joyce Williams

venison, his mind raced. His subtle efforts to draw on the family sympathies had produced results far exceeding his hope. He swallowed and said, "That's very thoughtful of you. I don't wish to impose, but you're all very persuasive."

They didn't need to know his sisters had disowned him for stealing the family ring off of their mother's hand while he was alone with her body at her wake. Or that he'd been at the Red Deer Inn for three days anticipating Nick's arrival. Or that his inquiry about local lodging was really a ruse to inspire Nick to invite him to Burg Mosel.

"Then we shall consider it settled." Lady Branden smiled at him before turning to her son and volunteering his services with diplomatic skill.

"Nicky, why don't you boys go riding in the morning before Jacques meets with your father? Familiarize him with the estate. Tell him a bit of the family history."

Jacques knew the glint in his eyes stemmed from a gratification far exceeding the pleasure of a morning ride.

* * *

Lady Branden rose from her chair, marking the

end to the meal. The weariness shadowing Nick's face prompted her solicitous comment, "You must be exhausted, Son." She turned to their guest. "And you, too, Jacques. Please, both of you, feel free to retire as early as you wish."

As they left the table, Lord Branden challenged Kitty to finish the chess game they'd started the night before.

Lady Branden speculatively tipped her head and narrowed her eyes as Nick and Jacques followed Kitty and Lord Branden toward the great room. Although neither young man would likely acknowledge it, intuition told her they shared a reluctance to let Kitty out of their sight. Amusement tugged at her lips.

Lord Branden positioned the game table in front of the fireplace while Jacques and Kitty secured four chairs from along the wall and placed them around the table. Lord Branden sat down and Kitty took her place opposite him. Jacques claimed the chair to Kitty's left, facing the hearth. Nick stirred the fireplace embers with a fire iron and then added more wood, prodding and poking until the fire crackled and the flames danced in shades of red, orange, and yellow. Lady Branden settled with her needlework in a small, low rocking chair near the candle stand and occasionally looked up to observe everyone.

Jacques broke the silence. "What a lucky thing for me you happened along just when I inquired about lodging, Nick." He sat back in his chair and deliberately scanned the room, taking in the elegant furnishings and accessories that spoke of wealth and world travel. "This certainly surpasses the comfort of commercial boarding." His gaze, resting on Kitty, held admiration so pointed that the color rose in her cheeks.

When Kitty lowered her bronze lashes and then flirtatiously raised them, Jacques responded with a playful smile that set the tone for the rest of the evening. One minute Kitty coyly hung on Jacques's every word. In the next, she laughed derisively at him over some nonsensical remark. The flickering firelight played over her delicate face; it shadowed her teasing eyes and enhanced each fleeting expression.

Lady Branden watched. Dumbfounded. Where did Kitty learn to play the coquette? Her mind leaped into action. Finding a suitable husband for Kitty had

weighed on her mind for over a year. Perhaps Jacques
. . ."

In the middle of her optimistic musing, Lady
Branden glanced up at her son. His burning eyes
stared at Kitty and he clutched the fire iron, white
knuckled. Confusion furrowed his brow. A muscle
twitched in his cheek.

Nick was jealous!

Raising Kitty as her own daughter and watching
Nick interact with her as a sister had made her family
feel complete. But tonight, Nick's interest in Kitty
clearly went beyond childhood friendship.

Unaware of Nick's distress, Kitty continued her
efforts to charm their guest. And Jacques returned
the compliment. The two of them laughed and
chattered, completely engrossed in their witty
banter.

So where did that leave Nick?

Tears stung Lady Branden's eyes. Must sorrow
always overshadow life's joys? Her heart surely had
already emptied its vial of grief; three small stone
caskets engraved with precious names—Anja,
Sabrina, Johanna—rested in the castle's burial vault.
Did heartache, like the biblical widow's cruise of oil,

never run out? Dear God, must she bear another cruel blow?

Resigned to the loss of her babies, she'd gone on with life. But the pain remained on the tip of her tongue, always ready with its bitter taste. And while she bore her own sorrows with grace and courage, to see her firstborn, the only child left to her, endure heartbreak . . .

Abruptly, as if physical action could relieve her disturbing thoughts, she laid aside her needlework and moved to the sideboard.

"Nicky?" she called softly.

He looked up at her, his distress instantly masked behind a cheerful smile.

"Help me with these, please," she said as she began filling the pewter goblets.

Nick returned the fire iron to its stand and promptly served the three who appeared happily absorbed in each other, but he shook his head when his mother offered to fill a goblet for him.

Although Lady Branden returned quietly to her chair, the tension around her mouth betrayed her serenity. Before she had time to pick up her needlework, Nick was beside her. He bent down and kissed her cheek, then whispered, "Goodnight, Mother. It's been a long day." The heaviness in his voice wrung her heart.

When Nick paused at the game table, the two men pushed back their chairs and stood. "Sleep well, Son," Lord Branden said, clapping him on the back.

As his father resumed his seat, Nick turned to Jacques. "Suppose we meet in the stable after breakfast tomorrow morning for that ride?"

I look forward to it," Jacques confirmed with a nod of his head before he sat down.

Nick stared down at Kitty's shining hair as he dropped his hand to her shoulder. Lady Branden watched his fingers almost imperceptibly caress the soft fabric of her gown as he said, "Good night, Kitty."

At the faint tinge of wistfulness in his voice, Lady Branden saw Jacques cast him a swift, assessing glance.

Without looking up, Kitty offered Nick a distracted good night and reached out to move her rook on the chessboard.

Lady Branden trapped her lips between her teeth and concentrated on her hands as she tugged at the snarled threads in her needlework. Unsuccessful, she finally gave up and jabbed the needle beside the knot. Twisted threads weren't the only snags that required time and patience to disentangle, and tonight she possessed a short supply of both.

CHAPTER FOUR

When the servants had finished clearing the breakfast dishes, Kitty spread the long table runner down the middle of the gleaming tabletop. As Lady Branden positioned the graceful silver candelabra in the center, she caught her husband watching her and met his affectionate gaze with a wordless invitation. He crossed the space between them and drew her into his embrace.

Kitty observed their interaction and respectfully shifted her attention to the window in time to see Nick and Jacques ride out of the stable.

As she watched them approach the low garden hedge and then follow the cobbled path that lead to the rear gate in the stone wall, her mind reverted to breakfast. Nick had barely spoken two sentences over

41

his millet porridge, and his face had looked tired and drawn.

Wrapping her arms around her middle, Kitty berated herself. Why did she notice such things? Why couldn't she stop loving Nick? She knew that pain would be the inevitable outcome of her feelings, but the power to control them eluded her.

"I hope the boys have a pleasant ride," Lady Branden's voice interrupted Kitty's dark thoughts. "Nicky seems so serious. Or maybe he's just matured."

There was no response; why didn't Lord Branden comment?

Kitty swung around only to discover she was alone with Lady Branden. She'd been so lost in her misery that she hadn't heard Lord Branden leave the dining room. She felt her face burn under the older woman's inquiring stare, and she stammered, "I—I'm sure I wouldn't know what Nick is thinking . . .

Feeling awkward over her unfinished comment, Kitty turned back to the window in time to see Nick and Jacques ride through the gate in the stone wall. While she struggled to regain her composure, tormenting questions darted through her mind. *Does*

Lady Branden suspect my true feelings for Nick? Is that why she's watching me?

A cold chill crept in to replace her blush, and she forced herself to take regular, steady breaths in spite of the wretched knot in the pit of her stomach. *Oh, God, what should I do?*

While she stared unseeingly at the snow-laden garden bench, her heart begging for an answer, she heard Lady Branden's departing footsteps.

Kitty's thoughts ran back and forth. She felt like an animal trapped in a cage. Even though flirting with Jacques last night had been fun, she'd seen the shock on Lady Branden's face.

Oh, will I never learn to behave like a lady? Must my lowly birth always jump up to mock me? Even if, by some miracle, Nick were to love me, could I ever really trust myself not to behave inappropriately in the future?

Luxurious surroundings and material possessions did not compensate for her inadequacies. Nick intuitively knew how to make pleasing and appropriate choices, but she seemed to lack that ability. She didn't belong in the scullery where her mother had spent her life; her shapely hands and

43

slender body were not fashioned for heavy work. But neither did she see herself as one of the Brandens. Oh, the fault didn't lie with them; they always treated everyone with the same thoughtful consideration. No, it was irrefutably her problem. But she didn't know how to solve it.

Admittedly, to convince Nick that she considered their kiss nothing more than an enthusiastic welcome, she'd responded too eagerly to Jacques's flattering attention. But she hadn't expected tension to accompany Nick's homecoming. His parents had lived for three years awaiting his return, and she'd participated in that anticipation, especially during the past few weeks.

After Nick's letter had arrived, with the promise of his return in time for Christmas, Burg Mosel's household servants had scoured the family living areas of the hieratic residence. In spite of the cold, they'd lugged every rug and curtain outdoors and beaten them thoroughly with wooden paddles to loosen accumulated dirt.

Each room, in turn, had undergone a complete scrubbing and airing, and when the mansion gleamed, the servants had gathered pine boughs and brought them indoors. Now the sweet aroma of winter greens permeated the rooms.

Kitty scurried from the dining hall, still wrestling with condemnation.

Only a few steps into the corridor, she experienced a strong impression—almost a voice: *Go to the chapel*. She cast a furtive glance over her shoulder, half wondering if someone had spoken behind her. As she crossed the vaulted foyer, she checked several more times to be sure no one was following her.

Just inside the chapel, she halted, glanced at the stained glass Shepherd in the lofty window, and then dropped a perfunctory curtsey in honor of Christ's presence. As her eyes darted around the dusky room, taking in the brightly painted saints that decorated the plastered walls and the rows of wooden pews that faced prie dieux for kneeling convenience, she berated herself for her foolish suspicions.

Taking a deep breath and relishing the resident aroma of incense, she moved up the aisle to the front of the little chapel.

When she reached the low chancel rail that separated the marble-topped altar from the nave, she

45

dropped to her knees, the skirt of her finely-woven dark brown wool *cotte* flowing out around her dejected figure. She rested her forearms on the rail, propped her chin on her hands, and closed her eyes.

"God, I have a problem." Her lips formed a whispered entreaty, "Please, I ask humbly, will You help me?"

The uncanny sensation of distinct words came again: *Read in the book.*

This time Kitty didn't look around for a messenger; she lifted her eyes to study the Book of Hours resting on the altar table in front of her. In the next moment, she shifted to her knees and then rose to her feet and skirted the railing. Catching up the large book, she pressed it to her chest. The book itself seemed to impart peace.

She slid into the front pew and knelt on the wooden kneeler as she placed the heavy volume on the armrest in front of her. The oval ruby centerpiece on the ivory cover sparkled at her from its gold filigree setting, and she slowly brushed her palm over the delicately etched vines and the flowers with pearl centers that surrounded the glittering jewel.

Then her fingers carefully released the hinged

clasp. Lifting the heavy cover caused the book's weight to shift unexpectedly. The colorfully illuminated pages scrolled sharply and fell open, exposing a pressed, dried flower. Wondering at the parchment-thin blossom's significance, Kitty picked it up and turned it over.

A yellow rose.

Why was it preserved? And why in this rare and precious book?

Perhaps she'd find the answer somewhere inside. She released a pensive sigh and gently placed the rose on the bench beside the soft folds of her *cotte* before returning her attention to the book.

Her eyes fell to the caption on the open page, *Hour Twenty*, and she instinctively mouthed the words as she read them.

> *I will lift up mine eyes unto the hills,*
> *from whence cometh my help.*
> *My help cometh from the Lord,*
> *which made heaven and earth.*
> *He will not suffer thy foot to be moved . . .*

Hope pulsed through her veins.

> *The Lord is thy keeper:*
> *the Lord is thy shade upon thy right hand.*

The sun shall not smite thee by day,
nor the moon by night.
The Lord shall preserve thee from all evil:
he shall preserve thy soul.
The Lord shall preserve thy going out
and thy coming in from this time forth,
and even for evermore.

"God, are you really watching over me?" Kitty's desperate question erupted from the depths of her being as she peered through her tears at the blue-robed Shepherd depicted in the sanctuary window.

She suddenly felt a strong kinship with the white lamb safely cradled in His strong, sheltering arms; it was as if she somehow knew that God would pick *her* up—just like that little lamb—and carry her securely in His arms.

In that moment, explicably reassured by the uncanny peace that engulfed her, Kitty closed her eyes. Time seemed suspended as she quietly basked in God's presence. She didn't have all the answers, but she knew without a doubt that God would help her.

When she suddenly became conscious of time passing, Kitty hastily picked up the delicate rose; searching for its significance would have to wait until another day, another time. But when one of the dried petals clipped the edge of the book's ivory cover, her heart clinched.

"Oh, no," her exclamation faded into a low moan as she anxiously rescued the papery blossom and settled it back on the parchment page.

Supporting the open volume with both hands, she lifted it, carried it back to the altar, and eased it onto the marble surface. When she picked up the rose to re-examine it, morning sunshine streamed through the stained glass window; it burnished her bright hair and filtered through the translucent petals of the dried rose.

Satisfied that the flower remained intact, Kitty released a relieved sigh and replaced it in the book. She closed the cover and fastened the clasp. Eyes downcast, pondering the verses she'd read, Kitty caressed the cover before straightening the book on the table.

* * *

The winter air, crisp and clear, gave frosty substance to their breath as Nick and Jacques rode their mounts, Chetak and Bohdan, single file down the winding descent toward the sprawling snow-clad

Joyce Williams

fields and ice-crusted river below. When the trail broadened, Jacques pulled up beside Nick and reined in Bohdan to match Chetak's pace.

Determined to hide his internal struggle, Nick fixed his eyes on the horizon. Last night he'd wrestled with his thoughts long after he'd gone to bed. Why did it disturb him that Kitty found Jacques so compatible? After all, he felt sure she understood that her lack of wealth and social connection precluded her from consideration for his wife.

So what was the matter with him? He should be happy for Kitty. If her acquaintance with Jacques progressed to marriage, it would mean financial security for her. Jacques, being astute as well as personable, would no doubt provide a stable living. Kitty really couldn't expect to do better for herself.

Then why had he felt slighted when she'd paid attention to Jacques and ignored him? If he truly cared about Kitty and wanted the best for her future, he should be eager to encourage her relationship with Jacques.

When Nick reined to a stop, Jacques immediately halted beside him and interrupted his tormented thoughts. "How much of this belongs to your father?"

Nick shielded his eyes. "Everything you see and that much again." He gestured with a wide sweep of his hand toward the smoke plumes dotting the countryside below. "See those clusters of chimney smoke?"

At Jacques's nod, Nick continued, "Fourteen towns and villages on our land pay tribute. Actually, everything really belongs to my mother because she was an only child and there were no other relatives to inherit."

"Hmm. Didn't your father inherit any land?"

The way Jacques stated his question made Nick bristle. His fingers tightened on the reins, but he forced himself to reply pleasantly, "No. He came here from Scania to aid my grandfather when a neighboring landowner threatened to attack him. My father conscripted the village men and trained them to fight, and they defeated my grandfather's enemy. King Sigismund knighted my father and commissioned his coat of arms. You might have noticed it hanging above the crossed swords in the dining hall."

Jacques nodded before continuing, "Tell me about your grandparents."

51

Nick pushed back his dark, wind-ruffled hair and gazed unseeingly over the landscape. "When my grandfather's two older brothers died young, he inherited everything. My grandmother came from England; my grandfather met her on a trip with his father. The canvas above the fireplace in the great room is her likeness."

Jacques persisted, like a doctor poking for a vein to bleed his patient. "Did you know your grandparents?"

"My grandfather." After a moment's pause, Nick shrugged and grudgingly added, "I never knew my grandmother."

Jacques raised his brows as he needled further. "Why? What happened to her?"

Nick managed to answer civilly, "She died when my mother was a child," but in the next moment he flicked Chetak's belly with his outside leg in a movement unseen by Jacques that sent him bounding ahead. He'd answered enough questions.

But Jacques was not so easily deterred. As they dismounted in the stable an hour later, he began probing again. "So, where does Kitty fit into life here?"

Nick dropped to the ground, took a steadying breath, and busied himself with affectionately stroking Chetak's face. In spite of his growing irritation with his guest, he mustered the self-restraint to answer matter-of-factly, "Her mother and mine were girlhood friends. When her mother died, Kitty became my parents' ward."

Although he felt sorely tempted to discourage Jacques with the bleakness of Kitty's socio-economic status, he knew it wouldn't be fair to her. But still, why did he have this insane urge to destroy any future between Jacques and Kitty? He, of all people, knew her best. Why, she was forthright, sassy, spunky, and brave.

He vividly recalled the ups and downs of their relationship. At its lowest point, he'd resented her seeming lack of gratitude toward his parents for their generosity to her and wished she'd never been born. Yet in the year before he went away to the university, they'd reached new levels of maturity and became close friends. Time had certainly changed that, he reflected sadly, recalling how she'd ignored him after that impulsive kiss.

* * *

When Nick's broad-shouldered frame filled the clerk's office doorway, Lord Branden looked up from the document in his hand. "There you are, Nick. Glad you could join us." He gestured toward a stool.

"Since everything I have will eventually be yours, I want you to participate in my plans." He waved the papers he held in his hand, "This is an application for a Hansa connection for the merchants in our largest village. If it is approved, we will participate in a cooperative distribution of goods with joint protection from pirating. Here, read it over and give me your feedback." He handed Nick the original document while retaining the copy.

The deference Lord Branden showed his son caused the bile to rise in Jacques's throat; how unfair that Nick should have so much and he should have so little. He swallowed hard and gritted his teeth before reminding himself that one day soon that would change.

While Nick read the document and father and son discussed the details, Jacques's thoughts took a detour. Frankly, his initial plan to connect with Kitty and awaken Nick's jealousy had already progressed better than he'd anticipated. This morning he'd pushed Nick to confirm the details recorded in his father's diary—but he didn't intend to jeopardize his welcome. Having successfully evoked Nick's jealousy, it was now time to play the gracious loser in the romantic triangle. Once Nick and Kitty were married, he would eliminate Nick. When Kitty turned to him for comfort, he would marry her, thus gaining what should have belonged to him by birth.

Lord Branden held out the signed documents. "I think that's it, Jacques," the older man's voice broke into his thoughts.

Jacques extracted a wax bar from his pouch and lifted it to the candle. Pressing his unusual ring into the soft blobs of red wax, he officially sealed the documents. He replaced the wax bar in his pouch before passing the original to Lord Branden and retaining the copy for his own records.

Their business finished, the three men moved into the entrance hall. When Nick's father draped his arm across his son's shoulders, Jacques paused beneath one of the canvas depictions of a dignified ancestors lining the walls and grinned in smug satisfaction. He could hardly wait for the next phase of his plan.

CHAPTER FIVE

Nick waited in his mother's sitting room while she donned her party finery with the assistance of her maid, Lenka, in the adjacent dressing room. A light rap on the door startled Nick.

"Someone's at your door, Mother," Nick relayed the summons in a loud whisper.

"Answer it—for me—There's a dear—See what—they want—I can't—come." Lady Branden's words jerked spasmodically while Lenka continued to tighten the laces down the back of her silk *cotte*.

The knock sounded again.

Nick opened the door and found Kitty standing in the corridor.

Color surged into Kitty's upturned face. "I-I came to ask Lady Branden to help me." She gulped, caught her breath, and stuttered awkwardly, "I-I'll c-come back l-later."

Nick stared after her as she fled down the hall like a frightened rabbit.

Lady Branden's voice came from her dressing room, "Who's there?"

"Kitty." Nick knew his reply sounded terse.

"What does she need?"

"Ah . . . she said she needs help." He began randomly rearranging the crystal goblets on the silver tray resting on a side table.

Lady Branden pushed aside the heavy burgundy and gold brocade curtain that served as a door between the two rooms and glanced around. She frowned. "Where is she?"

Nick felt heat creep up the back of his neck and burn his ears. "She left. Said she'd come back later."

Lady Branden's brows arched appraisingly at his mumbling. "Son, do we need to talk?"

His eyes flew to hers. Those words, common enough in his youth but quickly forgotten during his absence, brought memories flooding back. His mother knew him well. And their time apart hadn't changed that. He dropped to the nearby chaise, rested his elbows on his knees, and nervously intertwined his fingers.

As he looked up to meet her inquiring gaze, his frustration burst out, "Oh, Mother, I don't know what's the matter with me." He dropped his head and stared at his hands. "I watched Kitty invite Jacques's attention the other night, and I felt—I felt so . . . angry." He growled the last word. "I've looked forward to coming home since I went away. I guess I expected to pick up life here where I left off, without realizing that Kitty's of marriageable age now and needs to think about her future." He rolled his eyes in self-derision, adding, "Jacques would make her an eminently suitable husband. Even I can see that."

"So, why do you think you feel so possessive of Kitty, since you've just admitted it's irrational?"

"That's what I can't figure out." His exclamation ended in a groan.

"Did her behavior hurt your pride," she gave him time to consider, "or were you jealous of Jacques?"

"I don't know." His admission came out as a lament. "I wanted her to talk and laugh with me. Instead, she ignored me." He stared at his hands.

Lady Branden's eyes narrowed. "Do you,

perhaps, care more for Kitty than you realize?"

"No, of course not. I would never . . ." His vehement retort lost momentum as the real meaning of her question overtook his automatic defensiveness. He wiped his hand over his face in a gesture of distress that resembled his grandfather, Lord Schmidden.

"What shall I do?" He dropped his head into his hands. "Even if I did care for her, there could be no future in it."

"What do you mean?" Lady Branden's tone sharpened, "Surely you don't think we'd be displeased if you love Kitty."

Nick's head snapped up. He didn't bother hiding the accusation flaring in his eyes or the diffidence distorting his voice. "That's exactly what I think. I've known all my life that I must choose a wife from among my peers."

Lady Branden tipped her head to one side. "And where did you get that idea?"

Nick tightened his mouth into a sardonic line, but before he could speak she rushed on, "Oh, I know it's considered socially inappropriate to marry outside one's station in life—but surely you know your father and I don't feel that way. Kitty's mother was my best friend, and she was a scullery maid. And your father and I married for love when he didn't have a penny to his name. " Her voice rose. "How could you think we would expect of you what we didn't expect of ourselves?"

Catching herself in attack mode, she lowered her tone. "Kitty is a dear girl, Nicky. If you love her, I assure you, we would be very pleased."

Nick grimaced before he burst out bitterly, "Well, she seems quite taken with Jacques—so there's no need to entertain such foolish thoughts, is there, Mother?"

Lady Branden bent toward him, undaunted by his sarcasm. Resting her hands on his shoulders, she met his cynical gaze with a challenge in her own and spoke with conviction. "Jealousy is a dragon that will destroy you, Nicky. Stop worrying about Jacques and examine your own heart. If you discover you love Kitty, show her." She straightened and shrugged dismissively. "Now, you really must leave so I can finish dressing."

* * *

Just as Lady Branden raised her hand to knock

on Kitty's door, it flew open and Kitty burst out, barely avoiding a collision. "Oh, Lady Branden!"

Stepping into the room as Kitty rapidly retreated, Lady Branden offered, "Nicky said you need help."

"Well, yes, I did—I mean, I do," Kitty stammered, her chagrin flaming in her cheeks.

Determined to ignore the girl's embarrassment, Lady Branden swallowed her chuckle and dropped her eyes to the jeweled adornments she carried with her. Placing the necklace and earrings on the dressing table, she held out the headband to Kitty. "All right, my dear, let's see what we can do with this."

Positioning the impressive, marquis-cut amethyst on Kitty's forehead, Lady Branden eased the attached circlet of smaller stones down over Kitty's copper hair. She stepped back and tipped her head to admire the effect. "It definitely looks better on you than on me." She smiled and turned to leave. "Now, I must go check on Josef."

Kitty impulsively touched her arm. "Oh, I do love you, Lady Branden. Thank you." Kitty's thanks implied appreciation for more than mere assistance with the headpiece.

Lady Branden leaned close and brushed Kitty's cheek with a whispery kiss. "I love you too, my dear. More than you know." At the door she spoke over her shoulder, "I'll see you downstairs in a few minutes."

* * *

As Lady Branden descended the staircase, she recalled the scene she'd witnessed yesterday while standing outside the chapel.

Intending to spend time in prayer, she had pushed on one of the sanctuary doors and then glanced through the narrow opening before entering. Surprised to see Kitty standing behind the altar with her head bent over the parchment-thin yellow rose, Lady Branden had halted, uncertain if she should interrupt. But when a ray of sunshine suddenly streamed in through the stained glass window, engulfing the girl in golden light, Lady Branden experienced a sudden certainty that despite Nick's recent distress and Kitty's unpredictable behavior, God had a plan for their lives. She'd quietly closed the door and headed toward the staircase with a lighter heart.

Confident in her earlier impression, Lady Branden was able to put Nick's confusion and Kitty's awkwardness out of her mind. Worrying wouldn't change a thing, and besides, God was in control. And she had immediate responsibilities to think about.

When she reached the bottom of the stairs, she gave Josef last-minute instructions and sent him on his way to pass along the information to the appropriate servants.

Proceeding down the corridor, she poked her head in the dining hall to check on the servants assigned to set up the extra tables to best display the large trays of food and facilitate traffic flow. Satisfied with their efforts, she headed to the great room.

She glanced around the large room, noting with satisfaction that tall-backed chairs and several long benches had been retrieved from other rooms and now lined the walls, providing additional seating. Candles in the candle stands illuminated the space and blazed out a welcome.

The dissonance of strings in the adjoining music room resonated through the walls as the musicians tuned their instruments. Earlier in the day, servants had relocated the small room's furnishings and pushed the harpsichord back enough to provide space for the musicians.

Turning her gaze to the door as Nick entered the great room, she drew in a fluttery breath. The blue embroidery on his white collar and cuffs matched the brocade of his *tabard* and the blue of his eyes. The joy of motherly pride filled her heart as their eyes met in an affectionate glance. This handsome young man was her son! When he came to stand beside her, she clasped his arm and gave it a quick squeeze, but her throat was so choked she couldn't speak.

Jacques, wearing a black tabard trimmed with gold braid, appeared in the doorway. As he strode across the marble floor toward Lady Branden and Nick, he brushed his hands down the front of his torso in a deliberately nervous gesture. "I hope I'm dressed appropriately," he said as he reached them.

Tipping her head, Lady Branden observed, "You look quite dashing." But even as she complimented Jacques, she wondered at his expression—it seemed more a scowl than a smile—but when he turned to acknowledge Lord Branden's entrance, she dismissed her disturbing thoughts.

After a few minutes, Lady Branden glanced anxiously toward the door as she worried under her breath, "So where is Kitty?"

Ten minutes passed. Still no Kitty.

"Nicky," Lady Branden finally said, nervously twisting the ruby pendant gracing her throat, "go see what's keeping Kitty."

When Nick hesitated, Jacques shot him a quick glance and immediately volunteered, "I would be happy to go, Lady Branden."

Nick's jaw tightened. "Thanks, but I'll do it." He pivoted on his heel and strode from the room.

Lady Branden stifled a grin. She knew nothing motivates a man like a bit of competition.

* * *

Nick bounded up the broad stairs two steps at a time and then hurried along the corridor. When he reached Kitty's door, he tapped lightly and waited.

"Co-ming," her voice rang out.

He heard her quick footsteps as she crossed the floor in her suite. Soon they would be face to face. After her frantic departure from his mother's door earlier that evening, Nick wasn't sure what to expect. He swiped the perspiration from his forehead and shifted from one foot to the other. What was wrong with him? Surely it couldn't be that he loved Kitty.

Or could it?

* * *

Kitty extinguished the candles in the candle stand near the door with a long-handled brass snuffer and then replaced it on its hook. She reached up to confirm that her earrings remained in place. Although she'd been ready for the party for close to an hour, she'd stayed in her room, lecturing herself on the importance of behaving in a composed manner toward the two young men who'd so thoroughly upset her emotional equilibrium. Forcing her face into a smile, she gave her skirt a final smoothing and opened the door.

Behind her, darkness hung like a black velvet curtain. Light from the candle flames in the hallway sconces shimmered off the fitted bodice and gored skirt of her lavender silk gown. It struck the polished surface of the amethysts in her necklace, earrings, and headband, causing them to glitter like dewdrops on rose petals.

Blinded by the light from the hallway candles, Kitty lowered her head and squinted. Instantly, her head shot up and her green eyes popped open wide. Two hosiery-encased legs stood before her. Legs definitely not belonging to one of the maids!

Suddenly choking on her embarrassment, she closed her eyes and ducked her head. "Oh! Pardon me; I didn't expect . . ."

Ignoring her discomfiture, Nick took her arm. "It's only me—Nicky. You know, the arrogant boy who demanded you call him *my lord*."

Kitty was glad he couldn't see her flushed face, but the laugh in his voice banished her trepidation. They shared a hearty chuckle, recalling that long-ago day when Kitty had boldly defied Nick, refusing to pay homage to his adolescent conceit.

CHAPTER SIX

Lady Branden rang her silver bell, interrupting the voices of the young guests mingling in the great room. The clamor died down as everyone stopped talking and gave her their undivided attention. She extended a cordial welcome and suggested they find seats so they could comfortably enjoy the music of the troupe, Windsong, and then she watched with amused curiosity as they settled.

The curly-haired lad with the pointed nose and the rosy-cheeked girl wearing a brown velvet *cotte* sat close together on a bench and immediately began flirting behind her peacock plume while their chaperones hovered watchfully behind them.

The young man in the scarlet tabard leaned against the wall, his eyes fixed on a pale young woman who looked around appraisingly before she deliberately seated herself in front of the window where the dark draperies set off her golden hair.

Nick sat on Kitty's right on a green and gold brocade upholstered settee, while Jacques claimed the space to her left.

Everyone listened attentively as the musicians performed their first three selections, but when they paused to rearrange their music, Jacques turned to Kitty. "Do you play the harpsichord?"

She shook her head. "No. Musical talent is not one of my gifts." When Jacques opened his mouth to comment, Kitty quickly added, "But Nick plays beautifully. His mother taught him."

Jacques glanced over at Nick. "I understand your grandmother played too." Nick raised his brows but he didn't have a chance to reply because the musicians began another selection.

As the clapping subsided at the conclusion of Windsong's repertoire, Jacques leaped to his feet, announcing boldly, "I've just learned that our lovely hostess plays the harpsichord." He bowed toward Lady Branden with a grand flourish, sweeping the floor with an imaginary hat. "Come now, Lady Branden, please oblige us with a song or two."

Lady Branden demurred; it was obvious she didn't want to divert attention from the guest musicians. But when the members of Windsong deposited their instruments along the sides of the alcove and joined in supporting Jacques's request, she graciously conceded.

Slipping into her familiar place on the tall bench, she invited everyone to sing along as she played the carol *I Saw Three Ships*. When the last notes died away, everyone applauded enthusiastically.

Lady Branden stood and dropped a curtsey before she directed the musicians and guests to the dining hall, where a wide variety of delicacies awaited them: sweet tarts, meat rolls, cheese sticks, roasted nuts, dried fruit. There were "ooh's" and "aah's" as guests sampled first one tidbit and then another.

"Lady Branden, excellent party." As if to emphasize his compliment, the thin fellow called Freddie popped a roasted hazelnut into his mouth.

Lady Branden scanned the room, her eyes seeking Nick. She trapped her lower lip pensively between her teeth.

Where was her son?

She darted another glance around the room.

And where was Kitty?

A tremor of anxiety chased its way up and down Lady Branden's spine. Surely they hadn't slipped off by themselves.

She spied them then, just the two of them, standing in the corner, conversing with their heads close together. She took a step in their direction, intending to chide them for neglecting their guests, but a servant intercepted her with a question.

When Lady Branden looked back to the corner where Nick and Kitty had sat whispering, the bench was empty. Casting an anxious glance around the room, she saw them mingling with the guests and felt her panic subside.

A bit later, during a lull in the overall volume of conversation, Lady Branden again rang her silver bell. As the room quieted, she presented a request: "To honor the birth of the Christ Child, please join our family in the chapel for compline to conclude our evening."

As the jolly party guests made their way toward the chapel, the beckoning glimmer from the altar candles spilled down the aisle and out into the hallway, as if illuminating the pathway to heaven. And the stained glass Shepherd smiled on them as they filed quietly into the chapel and each acknowledged Christ's presence in their midst with a brief curtsy before finding a space in the pews.

* * *

Kitty was last to enter the chapel. She glanced around, pleased with the festiveness provided by the fresh greens she'd arranged the day Nick arrived home. Inhaling deeply of pine scent mingled with incense, she looked over the guests' heads, seeking a place to sit. Spotting an empty aisle seat beside Lord Brandon near the front, she moved toward the altar and slipped into the pew.

When she turned to look for Jacques, she discovered him standing alone in the back corner, almost hidden in the shadows. His arms were crossed over his chest and a grim expression clouded his face. Surprised by his defensive demeanor, she purposed to question him about it later.

Father Andrew's inspiring words diverted her puzzled thoughts as he came down the aisle swinging the censor.

Gloria in excelsis Deo, et in terra pax
hominibus bonae voluntatis. Laudamus te,
benedicimus te, adoramus te,
glorificamus te, gratias agimus tibi,
propter magnam gloriam tuam. Domine Deus,
rex caelestis, Deus Pater omnipotens . . .

Glory to God in the highest! Oh, will heaven be
like this? Kitty wondered as praise filled the chapel:

"We praise Thee, we bless Thee, we adore Thee, we
glorify Thee, we give thanks unto Thee, Lord God,
heavenly King, God the Father Almighty . . ."

* * *

Seated in the pew behind Kitty and Lord
Branden, Nick studied Kitty's face in the candlelight.
If there were no social impediments to consider . . . if
his parents approved . . . if that haunting kiss they'd
shared meant anything at all to her . . .

As his mother's challenge rang in his ears, *If you*
love Kitty . . . If you love Kitty . . . If you love Kitty,
Nick's tumbled thoughts gradually centered. Yes, he
was certain that he loved Kitty; had, in fact loved her
for a long time. He saw now that his socially
prejudiced mindset had blinded him to his feelings.

74

Nick leaned back against the pew. Loving Kitty explained his hurt feelings. And his anger toward Jacques.

And what was his mother's advice? Ah, yes. *Show her that you love her* .

That is precisely what he intended to do.

* * *

The concluding benediction marked the party's end. While the guests claimed their wraps, the musicians packed up their instruments. Several stable boys drove the guests' sleighs around to the front entrance where, amid much laughter, waving, and calling out their final thanks, the Branden's neighbors descended the broad marble steps and entered their respective transport.

The night sky shone clear, and a multitude of stars, like diamonds in a tiara, glittered above the old stone castle. A full moon beamed down on Nick and his father as they watched the departing guests pass along the cobbled drive. The faint strains of voices singing carols floated back from the sleighs as they vanished into the black velvet night.

Josef secured the heavy front doors as the two men, shivering from the frostbitten air, hurried to join the family, Father Andrew, and the musicians in the dining room, where they had all gathered around the fireplace.

Jacques stood at one end of the long table. "Grand party, Lady Branden. Your guests were so fascinating, I forgot to eat." He laughed easily and tossed a handful of roasted almonds into his mouth.

"I'm glad you had a good time," Lady Branden said, sinking down on a nearby bench.

When Kitty moved to the table and picked up an empty platter, Nick joined her, offering, "Let me help you with those."

Roused by his words, Lady Branden immediately stood up, chiding gently, "No cleaning tonight." She glanced around at the musicians and Father Andrew, smiling as she prodded indulgently. "Off to bed with you—all of you. It's late, and I'll see you in the morning." She gestured toward the door, good-naturedly ordering everyone out of the room

"You too, my dear," she said, smiling into her husband's eyes as he rose to his feet. She stroked his arm and added, "I'll be up in a few minutes."

When Kitty put down the empty platter, Lady Branden said, "The servants will serve us a late breakfast when they've finished cleaning up this mess." She scooted her toes into her slipper and gave her husband a light, affectionate push toward the door. "Off you go."

* * *

Father Andrew and the members of the musical troupe left the room first, heading toward their assigned guest quarters in the north wing. When Lord Branden moved toward the door, Jacques followed, catching up with his host at the door; their murmuring voices drifted back as they proceeded down the hall.

After Kitty departed, Nick wrapped his mother in an enthusiastic hug and bent his head to whisper close to her ear, "You give great advice, Mother."

She drew back, her brow wrinkled, her thoughts obviously still on the party. "What advice was that?"

"You told me to examine my heart. Remember?" he said, raising one eyebrow. "So I did," his smile warmed his face, "and things are much clearer now."

"Hmm." He had her attention. "By the way, what were you and Kitty discussing so intently in the corner earlier this evening?"

"I'm glad you reminded me." A quick, furtive

glance toward the doorway accompanied his whisper. "Jacques asked Kitty if she plays the harpsichord. She told him she doesn't, but she said you and I both play. Then he commented that my grandmother played." He frowned. "We wondered how he knew that. Did you tell him?"

"No, I've never mentioned it to him." Lady Branden tipped her head, "Remind me of Jacques's family name."

"It's Monet. He's French. But he said he's from Nuremberg."

"Really?" She reached up, unscrewed her left earring, and began massaging her ear lobe. Her forehead puckered. "A Frenchman called Pierre—I think his family name was Monet—lived at Burg Mosel for nearly a year. He taught my mother to play the harpsichord. That was a long time ago though. I wonder . . ." Her voice disappeared into her thoughts as she pressed her lips between her teeth.

"Do you suppose they could be related? That would explain his remark." Nick plowed his fingers through his hair. "But then why didn't he say so in the beginning?"

"It does seem strange, doesn't it?" She removed

the other earring and gently kneaded her right ear lobe.

Nick shrugged. "There's probably an obvious explanation."

He gave her another quick hug before impulsively kissing her cheek. "Wonderful party, Mother. I'm so glad to be home. It was great to see old friends. You're always so thoughtful."

"Thank you," she whispered, love shining in her eyes. "See you in the morning."

Nick strode down the corridor, across the broad entrance hall, and up the marble stairs. No light shone through the transom window above Jacques's door, but at the end of the hall, light from Kitty's window reflected into the hallway.

He tiptoed past the guest room and stopped at his own door, where he stopped long enough to remove his shoes before he tiptoed toward Kitty's suite.

Outside her door, Nick stopped and tapped lightly with his fingertips.

A long silence followed.

He waited.

Then just as he was about to return to his own

room, he heard Kitty's feet padding across the floor, and her anxious whisper came through the closed door, "Who is it?"

"It's me, Nick."

When Kitty eased open the door far enough to poke her head around it, her long hair, released from its combs, flowed over her shoulders in ripples like copper lightning.

A sudden longing to reach out and touch her hair swept through Nick with an intensity that left him speechless. He gripped the wooden casement framing the door and squeezed his eyes shut.

Although still soft, her tone grew sharp. "It's late, Nicky. What do you want?"

Startled by her brusqueness, Nick struggled to bring his senses under control. "Come riding with me tomorrow morning—early. I have something interesting to tell you."

"Oh, don't make me wait. Please, come in." She swung the door wide, innocently unaware of the beguiling picture she made, backlit by the candlelight.

Her jasmine scent reached out to Nick like a living thing, inexorably pulling him toward her. With great effort he sucked in a ragged breath, lifted one dark eyebrow crookedly over his twinkling eyes, and teased, "How can I refuse such a generous invitation?"

"Nicky!" Kitty's cheeks turned scarlet with the sudden awareness that they were no longer children. "You know I didn't mean . . ." His warm, low chuckle filled the space between them as she swiftly shut the door in his face.

"See you in the morning," he called softly, stifling a low, rumbling chuckle.

* * *

Kitty snuffed out the candles and then scrambled into bed, burrowing under the downy comforter. Would she never learn? How had she so quickly forgotten her resolve to treat Nick like a brother?

She growled her frustration and grabbed her pillow. Like an ostrich hiding its head in the sand, she slapped the silk-covered cushion over her face, hoping to cool her cheeks and block out the jeering thoughts that just didn't want to go away. She ordered her mind to think about the party, the guests, the music, Jacques . . . anything but the twinkle in Nick's eyes and his warm, low chuckle.

But sleep was a long time coming.

* * *

Upstairs in the master suite, Lord Erik Branden stretched out on his back in the canopied bed framed by wine colored velvet draperies that would be pulled shut when they were ready to sleep. Crossing his arms behind his head, he stared at the dancing shadows cast by the flickering candle flame on the wall beyond the footboard. When he heard his wife's approaching steps, he rolled onto his side and leaned on one elbow. As she entered the room, gratitude for a loving wife and for the years they'd shared flooded his heart.

"What a great party," Rosamund said, her happiness bubbling over as she approached him. "Everyone seemed to have such a good time."

As he scooted over so she could sit beside him on the bed, the dried lavender buds mixed in with the feathers in the duvet filled the air with their calming scent. He smiled at her and rested his hand affectionately at her waist.

"Nicky thanked me for the party." She sighed, "Isn't it wonderful to have him home?"

Even as his smile deepened at her pleasure, his mind reverted to something that had piqued his interest during the party. He tipped his head as he puzzled, "It occurred to me this evening that Nick and Kitty seemed—oh, I don't know, maybe my imagination was playing tricks on me—"

Rosamund fixed her eyes on her hands as she smoothed the bedcovers and questioned in a bland tone, "You thought Nick and Kitty seemed . . . what? "

"Well, they seemed to sort of, ah, you know—go together!"

Rosamund's eyes darted to her husband's; only when he was deeply moved did Erik struggle to articulate his thoughts. "You noticed?"

"Of course I noticed." Erik's brows rose quizzically and his tone intensified, "What do you know about it?"

Rosamund's pensive silence was followed by hesitant speculation, "We—ell, I think our son is struggling with the realization that he loves Kitty—"

Erik frowned and pressed his lips together before responding, "And that's—a problem?"

"Yes; he's not sure how she feels about him."

He stared at his wife in disbelief and snorted, "If that girl's got a brain in her head—"

He didn't get to finish because his wife

interrupted his indignant protest. "This is not a
matter of the brain; it's a matter of the heart." Her
hands flew to her chest. "Besides, Nicky thinks Kitty
might be seriously interested in Jacques."

"What!" Erik bolted upright, nearly bouncing
Rosamund off the bed. "Why, she hardly knows him.
And who is he compared to our Nick?" He knew his
voice grew loud, but he couldn't help it. "What do you
think we should do about it?"

"Shhh. Do you want to rouse the whole
household?" Rosamund's remonstration was offset
by a soft chuckle as she settled back on the bed.

She caressed his cheek with her hand and
commiserated, "I feel as you do about Nicky—nobody
could be finer. And we both want for him all the
happiness we've shared," her voice grew earnest,
"but don't you think it's better not to dictate these
things? Seems to me that interference usually
backfires. Let's trust that God, who brought *us*
together, will be faithful to our son."

As she leaned forward to kiss him, he wrapped
his arms around her, fell back against the bed, and
pulled her down close whispering fiercely, "I love
you. You know that, don't you?"

CHAPTER SEVEN

Jacques rolled over in bed and stared at the bright strips of sunlight sneaking between the shutter slats and marking stripes across the brass fireplace screen while his mind slowly reviewed the past few days.

The faint scraping of a key in a lock disturbed the stillness. Then a door clicked shut somewhere down the corridor.

Jacques sat up in bed, instantly alert.

Tiptoeing footsteps approached his room, implying that someone meant to move quietly.

Jacques flipped back the eiderdown duvet and dropped his feet to the floor. Plucking up a nearby chair, he silently positioned it in front of his door. With one hand grasping the back rail, he swung himself up onto the chair and grasped the transom window casement with the other hand to give him balance. Through the glass, he watched as Nick's broad shoulders and then his head disappeared incrementally as he made his way down the stairs.

Jacques glanced down at his feet, anticipating lowering himself back to the floor, but when he heard a second key grate in a lock followed by another set of softly tapping footsteps coming his way in the corridor, he gripped the window frame with both hands and leaned back as far as he could to avoid any possibility he could be seen. When the footsteps had passed his room, he quickly pulled his face close to the window.

Kitty.

He watched her reach the top of the stairs, her boots and *ushanka* clutched in her hands, and then she, too, slowly disappeared as she proceeded down the staircase.

Moments later he heard the distant thud as the back door shut.

He dropped to the polished wood floor, moved the chair to one side, and carefully opened his bedroom door. A quick glance in both directions indicated the corridor was deserted.

He crossed to the window overlooking the

courtyard in time to see Kitty dash along the hedge toward the stable yard.

He waited.

Within minutes, Nick and Kitty rode out of the stable together, confirming his suspicion that their meeting was pre-arranged.

Jacques's pulse leaped. Fate was offering him a perfect opportunity to test the information detailed in his father's diary. Lord and Lady Branden's isolation in a suite of rooms on the north wing's second floor made disturbing them unlikely, and yesterday he'd checked on the accommodations for the musicians and Father Andrew, and he knew they were safely settled in guest rooms on the north wing's main level. Now, with Nick and Kitty away from the castle, he felt confident he could safely explore without being discovered.

Back in his room, he dropped to his knees beside his trunk. He lifted the lid and confidently slid his fingers down the front inside panel. A shiver of anticipation shot through him as he depressed the small hidden button.

The secret compartment slid open with a soft little ping.

Jacques splayed his hands in anticipation and permitted himself a low, triumphant chuckle before he extracted the metal box containing his father's journal. He sat on the bed, forcing himself to inhale and exhale slowly; remaining calm and intentional was fundamental to his success.

He raised the lid, extracted the journal, and settled it on his knees. The small clasp that secured the leather cover was broken, so he easily opened the book to the section where his father had noted the location of Burg Mosel's hidden chamber. Drawing in a satisfied breath, he relished the acrid smell of old ink as he carefully reviewed the instructions outlining access. A hand-drawn diagram indicated that applying pressure to the side stone at the corner of the thirteenth step in Burg Mosel's tower stairwell would trigger the locking and unlocking mechanism.

He read through the procedure three times before he closed the journal. When it was safely stowed back in its metal casing, he replaced it in his trunk's hidden drawer.

After quickly shrugging into his clothes and shoes, he eased open his door. Following a quick glance left and right, he tiptoed noiselessly to the staircase, seized the railing for support, and leaned out to view the foyer below. Reassured that it was deserted, he hurried down the stairs, his ears alert for any sound.

As he passed through the vaulted foyer, he was confronted by the accusing eyes of one of Nick's ancestors in a portrait hanging on the stone wall. He clamped his mouth shut on his harsh expletive and pulled his gaze away.

"Revenge will be sweet," he reminded himself determinedly as he passed the chapel doors.

At the foot of the stone stairwell leading to the turret, he came to a stop. His eyes darted to the top and then swept back to the bottom.

One. Two. Three. . . . Eleven. Twelve. Thirteen. He counted each step under his breath.

There it was—the step that secured his destiny.

He paused again, listening for household activity. Silence.

Planting his right foot on the first step, Jacques started up.

At step eleven, he stopped. Sinking to his haunches, he studied step thirteen. He dropped to his knees on step twelve and reached out shaking fingers to touch the gray side stone in the left corner of step thirteen. Realizing it looked like every other stone and suddenly anxious not to make a mistake, he turned his head and again numbered the steps—just to be sure he'd counted correctly.

Eleven. Twelve.

Yes, this was it . . .

Thirteen!

Clammy perspiration glazed his forehead, and his heart nearly beat out of rhythm. He'd come this far, and there was no turning back now.

With his father's instructions firmly in mind, he placed one cold palm on top of the other and focused his weight behind his hands. Leaning forward and heaving all his force in one swift movement, Jacques lunged forward.

The wall's slow, scraping movement shot fear through his veins; the grating sound was far louder than he'd expected. Would the servants—or his hosts—come running?

Pinching his nose in response to the subtle wave of dead air that brushed his face, his gasp echoed in the gaping dark cavern that appeared before him. In his next heart-beat, a shocking idea struck him; he drew back, swallowing the gloating laughter that pushed up into his throat. His father had left him a legacy after all—a back-up plan!

The distant thud of pounding footsteps interrupted Jacques's perverse pleasure. They hammered down the marble staircase and echoed off the ceiling in the foyer.

Jacques stopped breathing.

The door leading down to the scullery smacked shut.

Sucking in a harsh breath of fear, Jacques pounced, this time slamming his weight against the stone in the corner of the thirteenth step. He held that breath for a heartbeat, and when the wall immediately began to close, he heaved a shuddering sigh of relief and swung around, eyeing the stairwell below him with desperate eyes.

Without waiting for the wall to settle back into place, he slid and skidded down the stairs. Righting himself at the bottom, he dashed past the chapel doors, crossed the foyer, and bounded up the marble steps, two at a time. At the precise moment his feet hit the landing on the second floor, he heard the door to the scullery squeak open.

When footsteps thudded toward the stairs, Jacques scrambled into his room, eased the door shut, and collapsed against it, panting and shaking with the panic and thrill of his narrow escape.

CHAPTER EIGHT

"I'll show you Prague: the magnificent stone bridge spanning the Vltava River, the royal palace, the astronomical town clock. And St. Vitus's Cathedral, a glorious work in progress." Nick's voice rose with his growing enthusiasm, "And the library—oh, Kitty, you can't imagine all the beautiful books." A faraway look filled his eyes. "And so many people with such diverse perspectives."

Listening to Nick talk, Kitty wondered if he would find their isolated life dull after the excitement of a big city.

"Were you sad to leave?" She raised her eyes from the snowy trail to look at his face; it would tell her the truth.

"Oh, not at all. Life at Burg Mosel is predictable and secure." He studied the peaceful countryside that appeared pristine in the early morning light, then stated reflectively, "All my burning questions don't seem to matter here."

"Burning questions?" The Nick she knew was always so sure of himself.

"Oh, questions about life, about the world and my purpose in it . . ." His voice trailed off as he stared at the deer stand in the tall oak tree where he and his father had sheltered many times and where he'd felled his first game, a six-point stag, the winter he'd turned eleven.

They rode in silence until a fox streaked across their path. "That's a sight I haven't seen in a while."

Nick's comment prompted Kitty's curiosity, "So—now that you're home, what are your plans?" She shot him a quick glance. "Will you be leaving again soon?"

He was slow to answer, and when he finally did, his sober reply shocked her. "My father has aged in the years I've been away." The tightness in his voice eased slightly, "I won't be aggressive, but I do intend to actively participate with him in governing the estate—so the eventual transition will be smooth."

She turned serious eyes on him and nodded. "It's hard to accept the fact that your father's getting old."

His shoulders slumped. "Yes, it is."

They fell silent as the trail narrowed along the river, forcing them to ride single file again. When the slight breeze ruffled the few crinkled leaves still clinging to the tree branches, Kitty tipped her head back and looked at the cloudless sky; no chance of snow today, she decided.

When the path again widened, Nick, who'd taken the lead, dropped back to walk his horse neck-and-neck with hers. Kitty turned and eyed him keenly.

"So, what is it you wanted to tell me?"

* * *

Sun-kissed copper curls peeked out along the edge of Kitty's white rabbit fur *ushanka*. Her cheeks glowed, rosy from the cold, and her eyes shone a brilliant green. Nick's pulse quickened; just being near her made him feel restless inside. But now that their relationship was back on amiable footing, he was determined to proceed slowly.

"After you went upstairs last night, Mother asked me what we were whispering about in the corner."

Kitty stiffened. Her eyes flashed and her mouth flew open.

Nick grinned and preemptively raised his hand

to keep her from interrupting. "Ah, ah, ah. Calm down." He knew her well. "I repeated Jacques's comment about my grandmother playing the harpsichord."

"And what did she say?" Just as he expected, eagerness eclipsed her indignation.

"A young man, she thinks his name was Monet—Pierre Monet, if she remembers correctly—lived at Burg Mosel many years ago." He glanced ahead at the trail and reined Chetak to a slow walk as he continued, "He was her mother's music teacher."

"Really?" Kitty's forehead creased in a puzzled frown. "But if they're related, why didn't Jacques say so?"

"I don't know," he paused, glancing over at her, "but I mean to find out." His tone had taken on an ominous intensity.

Kitty leaned toward him, "Oh, do let me help." In her fervor she relaxed her grip on the reins. "Maybe if I'm really friendly, he'll open up and talk to me." She looked down at the reins she'd nearly dropped.

Instant jealousy gripped Nick. His jaw tightened and he forgot his good intentions. "Not by my mother's honor," he barked.

Stunned by Nick's fierce antagonism, Kitty voiced her bewilderment. "Don't you want my help?"

"Not *your* kind of help!" The bitter accusation was out before he'd thought it through.

Her head snapped up and she gasped. "A-And just exactly what do you mean by that?"

"Just what I said," he shot back, his words biting, savage as a saw's teeth. "I watched you *be friendly* with Jacques my first night home. I'd rather not see that repeated."

* * *

Instantly stricken with burning shame, Kitty jerked on the reins and wheeled Bohdan, jamming her wooden heels into his flanks. Her startled horse fled back along the icy path at a breakneck pace. Crouching low, Kitty scrunched her eyes shut and squeezed the reins in her fists in a death grip. Her breath came in short, painful gasps, and her cheeks flamed as unworthiness again ravaged her soul.

In the stable yard she lifted her head and yanked on the reins, forcing Bohdan to skid to a halt.

Dismounting with more haste than sense, she caught her heel in the hem of her riding skirt, and in her struggle to free it, she dropped the reins. Bohdan swung his head around to look at his temperamental rider, upsetting Kitty's already tenuous balance. She cried out as she lurched sideways, pitched off awkwardly, and crashed on the frozen ground in a tangle of skirts and limbs.

As she fell, the ties on her *ushanka* came undone and it slid sideways, catching her crespine and dragging it from her head; both items of headgear sailed to the ground. Her bright curls, released from their confinement, sprang free and tumbled around her face and shoulders.

Hot tears burned her eyes, and she bit her lips to keep from crying out as sharp, vicious pain grabbed her right ankle and streaked up her leg.

* * *

Nick wrenched Chetak's reins and turned him about-face. Pursuing Kitty back along the steep trail leading up to Burg Mosel, he was startled to realize that the countryside flashing by had somehow lost its serenity. He charged into the stable yard in time to see Kitty lose her balance and fall from Bohdan. Flinging the reins over Chetak's head, Nick took a flying leap and landed, slipping and sliding on the frozen ground.

"Serves you right, running away like that," he reproached, dropping to his knees beside Kitty as he vented his frustration at her wild departure and his helplessness to prevent her mishap.

Tears plunged down Kitty's cheeks and splashed onto Nick's hands as he reached out to her.

Instantly regretting his churlish behavior that had impelled her to run away, he groaned and gathered her crumpled figure in his arms. But when her head lolled against his shoulder and her eyelids drooped shut, the sudden fear that stabbed his heart made his arms tighten convulsively.

Kitty's eyelashes fluttered and more tears rolled down her pale cheeks. "I-I'll be all r-right," she stammered, pulling away from him, struggling to sit up. "Ju-just give me a m-minute . . ."

Overwhelmed with relief that she was conscious, Nick plastered kisses on her damp forehead and wet cheeks between, "I'm so sorry," and, "Forgive me." He took her chin in his hand and paid no notice when she tried to jerk her head away. His lips found her mouth and he kissed her like a man in the desert seeks water.

Finally shifting his lips to her cheek, he

murmured contritely near her ear, "Forgive me, Kitty.
I should have asked."

* * *

Kitty's head was still spinning, but she had the
presence of mind to snap at him, "Why bother?"

Nick's eyebrows shot up and his chest rumbled
as he laughed—his low, exultant laugh that she loved.
"You're right. I'll never ask again." And as if to prove
his words true, he smothered any further retaliation
on her part with another kiss, and even though she
tugged to free her hands, he held her tight. This kiss
was warm and tender, and it left her flushed and
breathless and clutching his gray cloak.

Before she had time to collect her wits, Nick
abruptly held her away from him, startling her out of
her euphoric fog with an apology. "Here you are,
injured and freezing, and all I can think about is
kissing you."

She lowered her bronze lashes. They fluttered on
her blooming cheeks and hid her dancing green eyes.

"Oh, was I injured?" she feigned bewilderment.

"You . . ." His eyes lighted up when he realized
she was teasing him. "My common sense disappears
when I'm with you," he grumbled in the middle of a

chuckle. "But come, let me get you inside." Suddenly sober, his tone was anxious, "Do you think you can walk?"

Kitty momentarily wondered if her light-headedness and racing heart would affect her steadiness more than her sprained ankle, but she said, "I th-think so."

Nick collected Kitty's crespine and *ushanka* and handed them to her. Then he set her on her feet and supported her around her waist with his arm. But when she tried to take a step, her right ankle didn't hold her weight, and she sagged against him with a stifled cry. Instantly, he bent down and scooped her into his arms. Her russet curls spilled over his encircling arm as she hid her face against his chest and inhaled his woodsy masculine scent, savoring the moment, the fulfillment of her dream to be in his arms.

Carrying Kitty, Nick strode across the stable yard, along the hedge, and then through the inner courtyard to the seldom-used stairs in the far corner where the north and east wings intersected. He turned sideways so Kitty's feet would avoid the wrought iron arch framing the steps leading to the stairwell door as they passed through. At the top of the six steps he set her gingerly on her feet on the landing, but after he opened the door, he again lifted her in his arms.

Pale morning light filtered through the high window in the stairwell, highlighting dust moats in the air and casting shadows on the wooden steps that creaked under their combined weight. Tightening his grasp, Nick bent his head and brushed her forehead with his lips.

Kitty closed her eyes, certain that any minute now, she'd wake to reality—a reality made all the more cruel by the perfection of the dream.

Nick carried her into her room and deposited her on the bed. As she opened her eyes and blinked up at him, he commanded solicitously, "Don't move. I'll get my mother." He straightened up and dashed out the door.

Kitty sat on the bed staring after Nick as he disappeared. Pressing her hand to her lips, she swallowed hard several times. Trying to assimilate the morning's events, she leaned back against her pillows and stared at the ceiling.

First was the startling possibility that Jacques's

father had once lived at Burg Mosel. And then there was Nick's anger over the attention she'd showed Jacques the night they'd arrived.

Her thoughts leaped to her fall in the stable yard. Nick's scolding had stung her pride, but now she understood that he'd feared for her safety. And when he'd realized he'd hurt her feelings, his remorse had been tender and sweet. Her noble effort to convince herself he'd acted so concerned because he cared for her with normal brotherly affection had been short-lived; she'd even twisted her head away from him to avoid his kiss.

But when he'd kissed her, her heart—and her lips—had responded, despite her doubts and better judgment. She'd rested her head against his chest and wished with all her heart that the moment would last forever. Her unworthiness and shame, for that one glorious instant, were forgotten.

When familiar footsteps in the hall pulled Kitty back to the present, her mind raced with jumbled thoughts. What will Lord and Lady Branden think of me now? That I'm after their fortune and position? I have no family, no dowry, nothing to bring to a marriage. Caring for a penniless friend's orphaned child is one thing; having your son marry her is quite another. And come to think of it, Nick hasn't said a single word about marrying me. No doubt, my silly heart has exaggerated everything. Oh, what a fool I am.

Her taunting inner voice whispered, *You're trusting and foolish . . . just like your Grandma Hilde.*

She dropped her face into her hands and groaned in fear and despair.

CHAPTER NINE

"Oh, my dear! Nicky said you fell off Bohdan." Concern lined Lady Branden's brow and wrinkled the corners of her eyes and mouth as she bustled into the room. "Are you in a lot of pain?"

"Actually, it doesn't seem as bad now as I thought at first." Kitty bent her knee and leaned forward to slip her wool stocking down her right leg. As Lady Branden eased the material over her foot and tossed the stocking on the dressing table, she kept her gaze lowered; she could feel Nick's eyes on her.

"Nicky," Lady Branden said, her experienced fingers skimming Kitty's swollen ankle, "please order a large pot of hot water brought up from the kitchen as soon as possible." As he spun on his heel, she added, "Oh, and fetch the herb bag that's hanging on the chimney peg in my dressing room."

Nick returned shortly with the herb bag, followed a short time later by two servants cautiously carrying a large pot of steaming water.

"Place it here by the bed," Lady Branden instructed, "and be careful not to spill it when you set it down." When the cauldron rested safely beside the bed, she dismissed them.

Reaching into her herb bag, she pulled out a handful of pungent herb leaves and sprinkled them on the water. She tested the water with her fingers, but quickly withdrew them.

"It's too hot," she exclaimed, reaching for Kitty's water pitcher. When she'd emptied the contents into the cauldron, she tested it again.

"Much better," she said, swirling her fingers through the water in a circular motion. She watched the water until the leaves began to sink, and then she turned to Kitty.

"All right, my dear." With Lady Branden's help, Kitty shifted her legs over the side of the bed and eased her injured foot into the herbed water.

When Kitty was settled, Lady Branden patted her shoulder reassuringly, and then turned to her son. "Stay with her, Nicky, until Nora arrives." She tugged on the bell cord to summon the maid and then headed for the door. Nick followed his mother, closing the door behind her as she departed.

Then he crossed the room, caught up the straight-backed armless chair from beside the fireplace, swung it around, and plunked it down facing the pot of water. Straddling the seat, his arms crossed along its top rail and his chin resting on his arms, he stared intently at Kitty from under raised brows.

To Kitty's consternation, Nick didn't say a word—he just sat there. Watching her. She kept her head down and peered through the water at her foot, frantically searching her mind for something to say.

Twice, she raised her lashes a fraction and then just as quickly whisked them down again. Unbidden came the memory of his kisses in the stable yard. She bit her lip. She felt heat come and go in her face. Her uninjured foot twitched nervously. She knew if she looked at him, she couldn't help the love shining in her eyes. And it would be positively reckless and imprudent to expose her true feelings.

Finally, after what seemed an eternity, Nick tipped his head and inquired with a suspicion of laughter lurking in his voice, "Are you never going to look at me again?"

Her lashes flew up.

Their eyes met.

The burning intensity in his held her captive for a long, soundless moment, but she finally moistened her lips with the tip of her tongue and ventured with more than a little trepidation, "N-Nicky?"

"Yes, Kitty?" There was nothing hesitant or indecisive about him; his low voice rang full and sure and he looked her squarely in the face.

"Do you—must you look at me like that?" she blurted in the stress of the moment as she clapped her hands to her cheeks. "I-I can't think straight when you do."

"Look at you like what?" The mischief dancing in Nick's eyes belied his innocent tone.

"Like—like you can see right through me," she protested ruefully. Her skin prickled and she turned away from him.

Nick threw back his head and laughed.

A firm knock on Kitty's door startled them both.

Nick sobered as Kitty sat up straight and called, "Come in."

Without bothering to identify himself, Jacques opened the door. "Sounds like you two are enjoying yourselves," he observed dryly as he entered the room. His eyes narrowed, settling on Kitty. "From Lady Branden's report, I expected to find you half dead."

"Wha—at?" Kitty quickly hid her irritation behind a polite welcome. "Oh! Do come in, Jacques. Forgive my surprise; I was expecting Nora, my maid."

Nick jumped to his feet, turned his chair around, and offered it to his guest.

Jacques shook his head as he declined the offer, "No, thank you; I won't stay long," but his eyes made a slow perusal of Kitty's room, seeming to note every piece of furniture and bric-a-brac.

Kitty, feeling suddenly uncomfortable, tugged self-consciously at her skirt, pulling it down to hide her bare legs.

As Jacques moved close to the bed and peered down at her foot soaking in the pot of hot water, he suggested, "Lady Branden said your ankle will be better in a couple of days if you stay off of it."

Certainly, he meant to be consoling. So why did she feel reproached, as if she were a careless child?

Kitty pushed the thought away, ashamed of her criticism.

Jacques continued, "If you get tired of being confined here, we'll be glad to give you a lift downstairs." He swung his head around. "Right, Nick?"

"Right," Nick growled.

Kitty disciplined her grin. She knew Nick well enough to know he was wishing the suggestion had been his idea.

Approaching footsteps tapped on the hall floor, interrupting the tension of the moment, and Jacques glanced toward the door. "More company?"

"It's Lady Branden," Kitty informed him. "I know her footsteps."

The door opened and Lady Branden stepped inside, frowning as she observed the room's occupants. "Lord Branden is waiting with Father Andrew and the musicians for you boys to join them for breakfast before they leave. Zina enlisted Nora to help serve, but I'm sure Kitty will get along just fine without her until she's free."

"Happy to oblige, my lady." Jacques smiled at his hostess, nodded at Kitty, and promptly departed.

Lady Branden spoke over her shoulder while she plumped the bed pillows, "Before you go, Nicky, will you please scoot this pot of water out of the way so I can dry Kitty's foot and get her settled?"

Nick snagged the chair he'd offered Jacques and moved it away from the bed. Then as he bent over to grasp the heavy pot's lipped rim, he caught Kitty's eye and shot her a private glance that said *We're not finished yet.*

Smoothing the duvet over Kitty's lap, Lady Branden turned her head and deliberately raised her eyebrows at Nick, silently letting him know she was wondering why he had not departed with Jacques to join his father and their guests for breakfast.

Responding to her unspoken query, Nick addressed his mother in a low but determined voice, "Kitty and I were in the middle of an important discussion when Jacques interrupted us, and we need to finish it. I'll be down in a little while, but don't wait breakfast for me."

Lady Branden nodded at Nick and then reassured Kitty that she would return after breakfast. She went out and closed the door, and they listened to her departing footsteps tapping along the corridor.

"Now, where were we?" Nick grabbed the chair again and plunked it back down beside the bed. "Oh, yes, I know," he answered himself, his blue eyes laughing down at her. "You were saying I shouldn't look at you."

"That's not quite what I said," she protested, scraping her tumbled hair away from her face with her palms and clamping it at the back of her head, as if by restraining it she could control the situation.

"Oh, pardon me," his tone was audacious, bold, teasing. "What *did* you say?" he challenged, straddling the chair.

"I said . . ." she released her hair, sending it springing out around her face in an explosion of copper curls, "it's just that when—when you look at me like that—do you—I mean, what are your intentions?" Her heart sank; she sounded far too blunt.

"Intentions! What are my intentions?" The mischief lurking in Nick's eyes burst out into a self-satisfied chuckle. "I intend to kiss you, you little peacock."

He jumped up so abruptly that the chair legs clattered on the wood floor, but he impatiently righted the chair and shoved it out of the way. He sat next to Kitty on the bed, but when he reached out to encircle her in his arms, she resisted, pushing against his chest with both hands and averting her face.

"No. Wait, Nick," she begged breathlessly, fighting against herself, resolved not to let him kiss her again without having her questions answered.

Instantly, his arms dropped. "What is it?" Tender concern softened his voice. "Am I hurting you?" His brows met in a worried frown as he glanced down to where her injured foot lay hidden beneath the duvet.

"N-No, it's not my foot." She nearly choked on the words.

"Then—what is it?" Alarm squeezed his voice and drained the color from his face. "Are you hurting somewhere else?" He slid his hands along her arms, searching anxiously for broken bones.

"No, Nick. I'm fine." Her eyes pleaded with him, "It's just . . . have you thought this through? Do you know what you're doing—?" Her mouth went dry. Her head down, she addressed her mumbled explanation toward her chest. "Kissing me, I mean."

Nick abruptly grasped Kitty's shoulders. All traces of his laughter had vanished and he was utterly serious now. "Yes, Kitty, I know exactly what I'm doing; I've thought of little else since I came home." He put his finger under her chin, lifted it, and looked straight into her troubled green eyes. "I love you, Kitty O'Donnell. I always will."

Even though she caught her lips between her teeth and bit down hard, her chin still quivered. The Shepherd's reassurance that He would be with her, would help her, evaporated from her memory like morning dew as the voice of fear shouted loudly in her ears: *"Your grandmother had a baby out of wedlock and your mother was a scullery maid. You have no family. You have no dowry. You are not only poor, you are very foolish."*

Nick frowned, puzzled by her distress. "We've known each other for a long time, Kitty. Tell me, truly, what is it you're afraid of?"

Nick's gentle question interrupted Kitty's mental litany of unworthiness and shook her resolve. Hot tears prickled behind her eyelids, but she forced herself to ask the fateful question, "What about—" she caught her breath on a ragged sob, "what about your—parents?" Two giant tears rolled silently down her cheeks. "Do you really think they'll be—satisfied with me—for a daughter-in-law? Oh, I know they love me, but enough to . . . to overlook . . ."

"Kitty, Kitty, is that really what's troubling you?" Nick lifted one of her cold hands and cradled it in his own. He clasped it to his heart as his familiar, dearly-loved voice washed over her, low, warm, assuring. "Mother already knows I love you. She's the one who told me not to worry about Jacques—I was worried, you know." He pressed her hand to his cheek. "She guessed how I felt about you on my first night home. And she sent me to bring you down to the party. "

He leaned toward her, his voice growing stronger. "And as for my father," he grinned, the ghost of his youthful arrogance flickering across his face, "I know he loves you. But besides that, he loves my mother so much he'd do anything in the world to make her happy." He quirked an eyebrow quizzically, "But you surely know that by now."

While Kitty looked through his eyes into his soul, as if there she might read the truth she longed to believe, Nick's arms found their way around her. He held her close and lowered his head. His kiss was tender, reverent.

Then before she realized his intent, he slid off

the bed and landed on one knee beside her. He captured her slim hands in his strong ones and appealed earnestly, "Sweet Kitty, will you be mine?"

Kitty gasped for air, suffocating under the weight of fear and unworthiness that now jumped on her chest as long-term future implications of his proposal flashed through her mind: managing the servants, overseeing the food and drink for the household and stable hands, deciding domestic disputes, playing hostess for guests . . .

A flood of fresh tears blinded her eyes, and she groaned out loud as all the old pain of loss and abandonment gripped her by the throat, choking off her breath, making her words sound harsh and intense. "Y-You'll be sorry later. I mean, y-you should marry someone equal to you. And we both know I'm not." In spite of Nick's tightening grip, she pulled her hands free as she agonized further, "I'm penniless, Nick; I have no dowry!" She dropped her head in shame. "And I'm always doing and saying foolish things. I'll embarrass you—I know I will! And then you'll hate me."

Emotionally spent, the fierceness drained from her countenance. White and still, she scraped out a broken whisper, "I love you too much to do that to you."

Nick had scowled as her tirade picked up momentum, but when he leaned close to hear her final confession, his startled eyes grew bright with triumph. "Ha! So, you do love me!" With his next breath he declared vehemently, "And nothing else matters to me; not one whit!"

When Kitty kept her head turned and refused to look at him, the muscle in his cheek betrayed his inner tension as he pleaded his cause once more. "Please, Kitty, say yes. I love you so very much."

Caught between heavenly bliss and certain torment, she turned her head to look at him. Nick's pale face and the longing in his eyes moved her more than his words. But her deeply rooted pain and insecurity overpowered his pleading and her own desire. "Oh, Nick," she whispered, stricken, "I-I can't!"

He gave her a long, silent look before he sucked in a deep breath and wiped an unsteady hand over his face.

Kitty slumped forward, burying her face in her shaking fingers. Desperately, frantically, she cried out, "I'm so sorry; so sorry."

Although accustomed to getting his own way, Nick was also smart enough to realize that if he pushed Kitty harder now, he would back her into a corner. Resolve tightened his features. He slid off the bed and stood up.

"All right, Kitty, I'll wait. I want you to be certain of my love, of my parents' love," his hand gently smoothed her copper hair, "and confident in yourself." He turned and walked out of the room without looking back.

Kitty lifted tortured eyes and watched him go.

"Oh, God, what have I done? What will happen to me now? " she thoughts tormented her. She collapsed against the pillows, the hopeless victim of her paralyzing fear. She'd longed for Nick's love for years, yet when he'd offered it, her overwhelming sense of unworthiness had sabotaged her dearest desire.

Would she ever be free? *Could* she ever be free?

CHAPTER TEN

Following a hearty late-morning meal, the members of Windsong loaded their instruments and baggage into their sleigh and departed. When Father Andrew left shortly after noon, the household returned to a semblance of normalcy.

Nick volunteered to deliver the traditional Christmas basket to Arnold Werner and his family, the estate overseer who lived in the nearby village, so that Lord and Lady Branden could make the hour-long journey to pay their last respects to Letty, Burg Mosel's former cook, who lived with her granddaughter and was dying.

Jacques declined Nick's invitation to join him on his delivery errand, but after Nick and his parents departed, Jacques headed for the stable. A few minutes later he set out riding Bohdan.

Resting on her bed and nursing her injured

ankle, Kitty retrieved her down comforter and covered herself to ward off a chill. Exhausted from struggling with her tormented thoughts, she promptly fell asleep.

When urgent thirst woke her an hour later, strands of damp hair clung to her forehead and neck and perspiration glazed her skin. She sat up abruptly and threw off her cover, gasping as the cool air slapped her moist flesh.

A quick examination of her injured right ankle revealed that the swelling was reduced and her foot looked almost normal. She scooted both feet over the side of the bed, gingerly placed her injured foot on the floor beside her healthy one, and tried to stand.

"Ouch!" she yelped as stabbing pain shot up her leg. Sinking down on the bed, she sat there for a minute before again attempting to stand, this time with greater care.

Using her strong foot to hold most of her weight, she reached for the pitcher on the table under the window.

It was empty.

As she stared at it, she recalled that earlier that morning Lady Branden had poured the pitcher's contents into the pot of hot water to cool it down so she could comfortably soak her foot.

Her driving thirst brought to her mind the sideboard in the great room, where a half dozen pewter goblets and a decanter provided a constant source of refreshment. The back stairs were closest; if she took them slowly, surely, she would be all right. Of course, she should probably ring for Nora, but she felt restless at her unaccustomed confinement and rejected the idea of asking for help.

One cautious step at a time, Kitty limped along the corridor toward the worn wooden stairs. Several times she almost turned back, but her compelling thirst kept prodding her. Clinging to the railing and pausing on each step to rest her injured ankle, she managed to hobble down the back stairs.

Goose bumps popped out on her arms and legs as her clammy skin cooled, and when she reached the bottom of the stairs, she briskly rubbed her hands over the gooseflesh on her arms to stimulate circulation before she shuffled along the hallway.

Steadying her awkward gait with one hand on the stone wall, she made her way to the great room, where she immediately propped her hip against the sideboard to take the weight off her injured foot. Her whole leg now throbbed, and she chastised herself under her breath, *"You foolish girl, you'll end up in bed for twice as long."*

Tipping the decanter, she filled a pewter goblet and took several eager swallows, but her teeth chattered against the rim of the goblet, and a subsequent glance toward the fireplace confirmed her suspicion that the fire had gone out. She replaced the goblet on the service tray and scanned the room, looking for a silk shawl or wool throw to wrap around her shoulders.

When the heavy door at the back entrance creaked open and then thudded shut, the low reverberations resonating through the stone startled Kitty; instinctively, she turned toward the great room door. Living all her life at Burg Mosel, she knew the mansion's sounds, and because everyone's shoes had wood heels, she could easily identify the residents' footsteps. Lord Branden limped. Lady Branden tapped. Nick's long legs resulted in a smooth, rhythmic gait. Zina, the chief cook, stepped on her toes before her heels so she ker-lopped. Josef thumped. And Lenka's clubbed foot caused her to shuffle with each step—slide, step, slide. Dagmar's stiff skirts swished and crackled, announcing the head housekeeper's coming before she arrived. Matilda, the housemaid, skipped. The muffled pat of Nora's soft slippers—she alone refused to wear wood-heeled shoes—meant she often appeared without warning. And the lesser household servants—she knew their gaits, too.

Although Kitty listened intently to the steps in the corridor, the stride remained unfamiliar. Glancing out the window to determine the time, she saw that low-hanging clouds shrouded the rose garden and obscured the hedge, the stable yard, and the stone wall beyond in a thick mist. But it was still daylight. Which meant Nick wouldn't be back yet. Nor would Lord and Lady Branden.

As the unidentifiable footsteps grew louder, she puzzled over who they might belong to. Burg Mosel was an isolated community, and she knew everyone who lived and worked in it. Did that hurried tread belong to Jacques, the only stranger in their midst?

Filtered through her vulnerability, the approaching footsteps took on a menacing beat. Her pulse seemed to pump in her ears, and her hands felt

123

slick. Moisture beaded on her forehead. Whoever it was would soon be upon her. Knowing it was too late to escape, she glanced frantically around the room, seeking a place to hide.

Empowered by her fear, Kitty forgot her injured ankle and darted across the room. Hitching the fullness of her skirt between her legs, she squeezed into the hollow back of the knight's armor that stood to the left of the fireplace and raised up on her tiptoes to peer through the slit in the visor. Her heart thudded so violently in her chest that she thought her body would surely rattle the armor's breast piece.

When the ominous footsteps neared the door, she twisted her head in an attempt to see farther than the armor would allow, but the metal visor bit into the delicate flesh of her cheek and brow and made her wince. As the unidentified footsteps carried their owner into the room, her fear dissipated in a silent, relieved sigh.

Jacques.

Without even so much as a glance around the room, Burg Mosel's guest moved directly to the sideboard.

How silly of me to hide, Kitty scolded herself. *But*

now that I'm here, I'd better stay put. What excuse could I possibly give? Jacques thinks I'm an invalid confined to my bed. Besides, he's our guest, with every right to be in this room. I would certainly look foolish climbing out of this armor.

From her place of seclusion, Kitty watched Jacques pick up the decanter containing mild honeyed mead, their everyday drink. He sniffed it, wrinkled his nose, and replaced it. Grasping the decanter of elderberry wine, which Lady Branden had served the first evening of his visit, he threw back his head, exclaiming, "Yes!" But when he went to pour, his hand shook, and he swore impatiently as he had to steady the decanter with both hands to fill a pewter goblet.

Throwing the goblet's contents back in his throat in greedy gulps, he quickly drained it, refilled it, and drained it again. Without hesitation, he filled it a third time and downed its contents in three noisy gulps.

Kitty felt a twinge of alarm.

Jacques banged the empty goblet on the sideboard and raised his arm, drawing his sleeve across his mouth in an uncouth gesture as he belched loudly. Kitty raised her eyebrows behind the steel helmet. No family member or guest at Burg Mosel ever drank so much wine at one time—at least not to her knowledge. Lady Branden saw to that.

While she watched from her armored hiding place, Jacques straightened up, belching again, long and loudly, as he strode across the room toward the fireplace. Toward the suit of armor. Toward her!

Fear screamed in her brain.

Jacques halted only a few feet from her.

Please, God, don't let him hear me breathing, she prayed frantically, leaking out her breath one wisp at a time as she tensed her muscles to stop the shivering that gripped her—the metal seemed to have absorbed the room's chill, and its silver smoothness burned like ice against her bare skin.

Of course, she could just pop out and laughingly confess her foolishness. After all, Jacques had done nothing to arouse such outrageous fear. Even if he'd had a bit too much to drink, surely, he was harmless.

While she reproached herself for allowing her run-away imagination to put her in such an absurd predicament, Jacques raised his head and stared boldly at the canvas portrait of Nick's grandmother, Lady Rose, mounted above the fireplace. In the next moment, he addressed the pictured woman in a strident taunt that curdled Kitty's blood.

"Scorned my father, did you? Thought you were too good for him. Rejected him and sent him away. Cast him aside like rubbish."

Kitty struggled to make sense of Jacque's irrational tirade. What did he mean, saying that Lady Rose had scorned his father?

"He saw to it that you got what you deserved, didn't he?" Hands on his hips, Jacques flung the vengeful words at the canvas and stomped his foot.

The sharp click of his wood heel on the stone floor covered Kitty's horrified gasp, but fear that he'd heard her shot her heart into her throat. She clenched her teeth together so tightly to keep them from chattering that her jaws ached.

"Gullible Nick, I fooled him. Ha! I fooled them all."

Could that caustic voice really belong to the same person who'd been their charming guest for nearly a week?

"And now your spoiled grandson wants to marry the red-head—so all is working out like I'd planned."

His short laugh was as frightening as his confession was shocking.

Indignation rose up in Kitty. Nick, spoiled? Why, of all the nerve! Of course life's advantages had been Nick's. That was how it should be. After all, Nick was heir to Burg Mosel, and his self-confidence only increased his attractiveness. Besides, who would respect him if he cowered?

But Jacques's insanity did not stop for her thoughts. "When I've disposed of him, who better than me to rescue the poor girl from her widow's grief?"

Kitty's ears rang. Unconsciously, she held her breath, afraid even to blink lest Jacques would sense the movement. Tears stung her eyes and trailed silently down her face.

Jacques shook his fist in a violent gesture at the woman on the canvas before swinging his opened palm inclusively around the room. "Then this will all be mine. You hear? All mine." He swung on his heel and returned to the sideboard, where he poured himself yet another refill.

When the decanter was empty, he swore viciously at the portrait of Lady Rose, and his distorted face reminded Kitty of the gargoyles on Burg Mosel's drain spouts.

Interrupting her thought, Jacques slammed the goblet down on the sideboard with a loud thump. The service tray, empty decanter, and additional goblets bounced and clattered.

And in the armor, Kitty jerked.

Some of what Jacques had said didn't make sense, but Kitty was now certain that he'd come to Burg Mosel intending to charm his way into their confidence and promote a marriage between Nick and her that would end with Nick's death. Since there were no other heirs, she would inherit everything. He would then console her and marry her, thereby gaining control of the Branden's property.

As her thoughts progressed, perspiration formed on Kitty's forehead, chin, and nose, and rivulets trickled down her back and legs. But the discomfort she felt was minor compared to the terror generated by the confession she'd just witnessed. She cast a silent prayer heavenward: *Dear God, what should I do? Tell Lord Branden? Would he believe me? The whole idea is too bizarre; I wouldn't believe it myself if I hadn't heard it with my own ears.*

When a bead of moisture tickled her nose, Kitty had a sudden compulsion to sneeze. Desperate, she scrunched up her face—but she was too late to prevent the loud "Ker-choo!" that reverberated inside the armor. Opening her eyes, she peered out of the mask. Jacques was lurching toward her. Terror distended her ribs and pushed up to close her throat.

But in spite of her panic, she clung to her presence of mind. Deciding her best option was to brazen her way out of the awkward situation, she sucked in a bracing breath and boldly stepped out of her hiding place.

"Surprise," she declared, pasting a bright, amused smile on her face. "What were you saying about planning a marriage between Nick and me? Come now," she infused her words with humor, "I really thought that was our idea."

Jacques started as if he'd seen a ghost. Then in the next instant, like a looming predator, he closed the space between them. "So, you were listening." Up close, his eyes glittered cold and hard. "And I just bet I know what you're thinking; you're thinking you'll thwart my plans and refuse to marry Saint Nick." He gave a short laugh at his own joke.

But when she joined him, hoping her laughter would lighten his mood, his eyes narrowed to malevolent slits. "You listen well; if you don't marry angel boy, you won't be marrying anybody." His threat ended in a menacing growl, "Not ever."

Kitty's body quivered from fear and cold, but she forced herself to hold her ground; she was fighting for her life. She flouted sarcastically, "That would defeat your purpose, wouldn't it?" Clenching her hands behind her back to steady her shaking arms, she teased, "If I remember right, there are still several torture machines in the dungeon. Maybe you want to stretch me on the rack. What do you think? Would that make me cooperate?" She tipped her head provocatively, still smiling.

When Jacques did not respond to her humorous exaggeration, desperation drove her to continue. "No, no, I have a better idea. A few drops of poison for dear Saint Nick. Now, that would do the trick, wouldn't it? Easy. Painless." She dropped her voice to a confiding whisper, "And no one would know." Her soft, derisive chuckle was a deliberate triumph over fear. "Except me. And of course I'd be too afraid not to cooperate, don't you think?"

With a final show of bravado despite the cold smell of fear filling her nostrils, she lifted her chin and sneered, "But you couldn't be sure, now, could you? I just might tell the Brandens all about you and your diabolical plans."

Like a wild animal pouncing on its prey, Jacques lunged at Kitty.

She thrust out her arms to push him away but fear drained the blood from her head. The kaleidoscope of stars tumbling in her eyes threw her off balance. Her weak ankle twisted.

Grimacing, Kitty directed her pain into bold defiance, "God will save us!"

Jacques laughed. An ugly cackle. And his vile breath triggered a wave of nausea that stripped her of strength. He reached out, crushing her throat in his hot, wicked hands.

Fright dilated Kitty's eyes. She sucked a gasping breath but no air would come. And his fingers blocked her scream.

Down she went. Sucked into quiet, murky darkness.

CHAPTER ELEVEN

Kitty struggled to think. Her bed felt as hard as stone. And she was cold. So cold. Her throat burned and her head pounded like a smithy's hammer. Oh, where was her satin cushion? And her duvet?

She slowly opened a clenched fist and stretched her stiff, aching fingers. When she thrust out her hand, reaching for her comforts, there was only cold stone.

Think, Kitty, think, she prodded herself, too miserable even to groan. Her mind refused to cooperate. Thinking had never been this painful. She gave in to the seducing blackness.

But something deep inside of her kept forcing her to surface, and she floated in and out of consciousness several times before she wondered where she was. With great effort she concentrated on reviewing Burg Mosel, building by building, room by room. The armory? No, it smelled of tallow and leather. The spinning chamber? No, carding and spinning dust always made her sneeze. The smithy? No, surely she would recognize the acrid odor of hot iron. The scullery? It stank of human sweat and soured food. The tower? It was never completely dark because the windows had no shutters.

If only my head didn't hurt, she thought, reaching up to touch the spot that throbbed. She winced when her exploring fingers discovered a lump as large as a goose egg behind her right ear.

So where—?

The dungeon. Could this be a room in the dungeon? It certainly smelled dank. Like cold, underground stone. She struggled to recall Burg Mosel's lower vault; she'd only been down there once. But how . . . no, the dungeon had a dirt floor.

She touched the algid stone beneath her body—again—just to be sure . . .

Oh, God, where am I?

A tremor rippled up and down her spine. Could it be . . .?

No, it couldn't be.

Or could it?

But how . . . ?

Think harder, Kitty, she goaded herself in ruthless desperation.

Gradually, bits and pieces of memories began to float back into her mind. Some thoughts were distinct. Others were more elusive, mere phantoms of ideas.

The smell of sour wine. When he—when he—?

Her thoughts compelled her up onto one elbow.

Rubbing her eyes with her free hand, she tried to scrub the confusion from her mind.

Oh, yes. Jacques.

When Jacques—when Jacques choked me!

She opened her mouth to scream, as if there had been no time lapse. But the pain in her throat strangled her scream. She clutched her neck and sucked in thin, wheezing breaths of cold, stale air.

With concentrated effort, she forced herself to relax, and when her breathing was finally normal again, her thoughts picked up speed, darting from question to question. Where is Jacques? Did *he* put me here? But how could Jacques know about . . . ?

Only the family and the servants knew . . . and nobody ever gave it a thought.

The relentless drumming in her head sabotaged her ability to reason. She slumped back down onto the cold stone, struggling to hang onto consciousness.

Then free-falling in that space between sense and oblivion, her thoughts played leapfrog: Jacques said Nick's grandmother had gotten what she deserved. What did that mean? What did she deserve?

Kitty shuddered convulsively—and not just from the cold. She saw it clearly now; Lady Rose's death had not been an accident. The blood pounded loudly against her temples as she realized that Nick's grandmother had been murdered!

She sat up, clutching her head and muttering, "What does that have to do with me, Kitty O'Donnell, a penniless orphan? Why would I be put in the hidden cha . . . oh, no!" A painful spasm squeezed her throat and she eked out strained words, "I wouldn't cooperate with Jacques, so he meant to kill me. Just like his father killed Lady Rose by imprisoning her in the secret chamber . . ."

Bending from her waist, Kitty cradled her

throbbing head with her palms and massaged her scalp with her fingertips. Fear for herself was no longer her only consideration. She knew where she was. And why. But there was no telling what Jacques might decide to do, now that he believed her to be out of the way.

Concern for Nick and his parents gripped her heart. Oh, if only I knew how long I've been here, she wished frantically. Then recognizing the futility of wishing, she prodded herself to hang on to her wits and find a way to escape.

She rolled over onto her thinly clad stomach, instinctively recoiling from the cold stone. But desperation gave her determination. When she shifted slowly to her hands and knees, stars danced in her eyes, forcing her to hang her head until the sensation subsided.

But she refused to give up.

Extending her fingers like a cat's whiskers, she inched forward, crawling through the darkness. When she bumped into a stone wall, she ran her hands, palms flat, up the wall and back down and then from side to side. Yes, she concluded, there could be no doubt—she was in the secret chamber.

Slowly shifting to her knees, Kitty lifted her right leg and placed her bare foot on the cold floor. But when she attempted to stand, searing pain shot up her leg. Her body started to shake. She leaned her head against the wall and wrapped her arms around her middle in an effort to control the shaking. How could she have forgotten her injury?

After several seconds, the pain subsided to a dull throb. Lifting her left knee and supporting her weight on her strong left ankle, she pushed her body to a standing position. Yes, she was upright!

She leaned against the wall, resting her weight on her left leg. Propping the bare toes of her dangling right foot on the top of her left foot, she paused to consider her situation. There must be a way out of this tomb. She shuddered at the thought, but there was no denying that's what it was; Nick's grandmother had died in here. Her hope of escape defied common sense.

But she had to try—she couldn't just sit down and wait to die.

She opened her eyes wide, then squinted intently, but her sight served no purpose in the inky blackness; she would have to rely on her sense of touch. With her hands extended at waist level, she began methodically brushing them over the stone wall in a circular pattern. If I cover every square inch of this place, she reasoned, maybe I'll discover *something*.

She took shuffling steps, putting as little weight as possible on her aching ankle while she repeated the searching movements.

Palming the implacable stone sent shivers spiking through her whole body. "I will not give up," Kitty promised herself then gritted her teeth in defiance against her longing for oblivion. "I must find a way to warn Nick."

Despite her determination, her hands moved more and more slowly. She felt her arms go slack— and then her body collapsed. When her left hand struck out in a feeble attempt to prevent her fall, the sharp edge of a protruding stone snagged her tender skin. A burning sensation tore through her hand in the instant before she crashed to the cold stone floor.

Ouch! Her senses surged into full alert. She raised her stinging hand to her mouth. Hot and wet. Blood! Why, oh, why hadn't she been more careful?

And then it struck her: Only an irregularity in the

surface of the stones would tear her skin. Hope tugged at her heart.

She clenched her teeth and repeated the painful process of getting back on her feet. And wondered how soon the cold would numb the pain.

She again ran her hands over the smooth wall, moving them inch-by-inch. The stones all fit together seamlessly. Then she caught her breath. In spite of the frigid air in the cavern, her body flushed hot with excitement.

Yes! The irregularity was a mere fraction—but it could mean the difference between life and death.

Tracing a slim finger around the slightly raised edge, she felt nothing else, no indentations, no other variances. She rapped the knuckles of her right hand along the wall to the right and then to the left, listening. The echo sounded the same on both sides.

Placing her fingertips along the protruding stone's narrow sides, she pulled on it. But the edges were sharp, and there wasn't enough substance to afford a good grip. Her fingers slipped. She lost her balance and staggered backwards, crying out as stabbing pain shot up her right leg.

When she'd regained her balance and allowed

her panic to subside, she tried again. This time she positioned her index fingers under the stone's lower edge with the backs of her remaining fingers flat against the wall and her palms facing her belly. Bending her knees and concentrating all her strength in her wrists, she heaved upward. Her fingers slipped off the narrow extension and her knuckles scraped over the stone and up the wall. But nothing moved. She clutched her hands to her chest, rubbing one inside the other to ease her smarting knuckles.

Resolutely, she straightened up and repositioned her hands with her thumbs on the stone's narrow upper corners, her open hands extending down along each side. Rising up on tiptoe, she leaned in and bore down along the upper ledge, grunting as she transferred her body weight onto her thumbs.

Again, nothing.

Exhausted, battling the insidious pull of sinking despair and depleted oxygen, she propped her forehead against the cold stone wall and pressed the still-bleeding wound against her mouth.

Suddenly she lifted her head, whispering, "I could push in on the stone. Why didn't I think of that first?" Infused with new hope, she splayed her hands on the cold wall and passed a few broad sweeps across the surface to relocate the protruding stone. When her stiff fingers finally identified it, she palmed the stone and stacked her hands. Focusing all the desperation of her body and soul into her hands, she tensed and leaned in with a mighty push, crying, "Please, God, help!" It was a final, frantic effort.

Nothing moved.

Kitty slumped against the wall. That stone had been her only hope. Like an out-of-body experience, she knew her body slid down the wall and she knew her head bumped against the stones several times—but she was powerless to react. She landed in an unconscious heap, unaware that the wall had begun to shift.

Blocks of stone ground against each other. Then a section of the wall swung open. When an icy blast of fresh air slapped Kitty's limp form, her body twitched. She shuddered and then coughed, which increased the pressure in the bumps on her head. Pain became her friend, forcing her to consciousness. And with it came the realization that rushing cold air could only mean one thing: an outside source.

"Oh, thank you, God," she wheezed, still stunned

that the imprisoning chamber wall had actually moved.

She gulped in great breaths of frigid air and stared into darkness; the wall had not opened into the familiar tower stairwell in Burg Mosel! As her brain screamed, *Where am I?* fear bolted along her spine and sent panic pulsing to every limb.

Kitty rolled to her knees, lifted her head, and sniffed. But the dankness of cold stone offered no clues. Her parched tongue scraped over her dry lips before she sucked them in between her teeth. This was a new challenge—requiring more determination.

"I need help, God," seemed to be the only thing worth saying.

Poking out cautious fingers, she tentatively investigated the perimeters of the opening in the wall. Smooth stone blocks seamlessly fit together to form a doorway, and the stone floor that stretched out as far as she could reach suggested a passageway.

Again exercising deliberate care, she rose to her feet and continued her blind exploration.

Determining that the doorway was tall enough to pass through without bending over, she took one tentative, limping step into the opening. But when her injured foot, hesitantly extended for the next step, pawed vacant air, only her frantic grab at the stone doorframe saved her from a forward plunge. Her supporting leg wobbled, threatening to buckle under her.

She started to cry.

Swiping at her gushing tears with the heel of her hand, she sniffed and tried to swallow the lump that had lodged in her throat while she considered what the end of the floor might mean. Was this a cruel trick? A sadistic joke? Maybe she'd discovered an old well? Or perhaps this hole hid evidence of—murder? Or . . . maybe . . . could it be . . . a stairwell leading to an exit?

"Oh, please, God, let there be steps," Kitty petitioned through her chattering teeth.

Using the smooth stones framing the opening as a reference point, she lowered herself to the floor and squeezed her eyes tightly closed; when they were open, she concentrated on trying to see into the inky blackness, but right now she needed to focus on touch. Cautiously curling her hand over the abrupt edge of the floor, she reached down a bit. And a little bit more.

"Yes," she sobbed, blinking hard to clear away tears of relief when her fingers identified a step.

As she shifted to a sitting position, the cold stone triggered spasms of trembling. She wrapped her arms around her torso and admonished herself through chattering teeth, "You can do this, Kitty. You must save Nick."

With one hand on the stone wall, Kitty slowly scooted on her bottom down one icy stone step at a time. She forced herself to repeat the testing process with her feet—despite her curled toes that hesitated to touch what she couldn't see.

When a desire to hurry pressed her to the brink of madness, she buried her head between her knees and ruthlessly reminded herself that one wrong move could easily send her pitching down into the dark unknown below—and there was no one to rescue her if she had an accident. Furthermore, there was no way to know what awaited her at the bottom.

But her mind did not lack for ideas. Snakes. Rats. Bats. Bones. She shook her head to clear away her gruesome imaginings.

And then, after sixty-four steps—she'd counted each one—the stairway abruptly ended and the stones again became a floor, a floor of roughly hewn stones separated by dirt.

Kitty clung to the wall for support and carefully rose to her feet, still blind in the darkness. With the wall as her only guide, she was afraid to guess where it might end, so after every few steps she paused and opened her eyes, straining to see. And each time, still in darkness, she bent down and explored the floor ahead for obstacles and confirmed that the wall continued.

Even though inching along the lengthy passage seemed to take forever, her sprained ankle no longer hurt because the frigid air had numbed her feet and legs.

She shivered violently. Did the air seem to be growing colder?

She opened her eyes.

And blinked.

And blinked again.

Was that—could it be? She pressed her fingers against her closed eyelids before she dropped her hands and looked again.

Yes, there was a faint vertical sliver of light. A dangling thread of hope.

She blinked again. No, it was not the delusion of her desperation or her imagination.

Courage pumped through her veins, prompting her to shuffle faster as she neared the light.

Lacking warm clothing or shoes, Kitty's body shook with a chill, but her fierce determination to warn Nick remained stronger than her discomfort or fear.

"I can do this. I can do this," she chanted fiercely through her chattering teeth. "One more step. One more step."

By the time she reached the sliver of light, her heart was thumping so strongly in her chest that she was panting. She drew in a bracing breath and then, with her belly sucked in tight, she forced her slender body sideways through the narrow slit.

Popping out into fading daylight, she stared around, stunned. The tunnel twisted back on itself and ended abruptly in a cave. Frosted bushes and tangled, ice-sheathed vines formed a web over an opening about two feet above her head, and snow had filtered down and lay in shallow drifts along one side of the cave hollow.

When she and Nick were children, they'd often

played on the hillside outside the castle. One cloudy day she'd fallen through the thorny wild blackberry bushes obscuring a cave's entrance. Maybe this cave's entrance? She instinctively buffed her arms with her stiff hands, remembering the tumble and the scratches she'd suffered.

"Aha," burst from Kitty's lips when she spied the long stick Nick had used all those years ago to clear the opening so he could climb in after her without getting badly scratched. Once inside, the two of them had explored as far as daylight reached, but the sharp twist in the tunnel and the narrow slit and the darkness beyond had prevented them from venturing very far. And once they'd managed to climb out of the cave, the harsh thorns had dissuaded them from ever climbing back in.

It was incredible to think this cave's secret had been here all the time. No one had ever mentioned stairs and a tunnel leading from the secret chamber to the outside. Could that mean that nobody knew about it? And now, here she was, standing in the snow below the cave's entrance, peering up into the rapidly fading twilight.

"Oh, please, God, let me be in time to intercept

Nick or his parents on their way home." She ended her plea in a ragged cry, "God, I need Your help."

With a surge of faith—after all, her escape was a miracle, wasn't it?—she grabbed Nick's long stick and attacked the icy brush that screened the cave's opening.

Loosened frost and snow cascaded down into the cave, showering her face and arms with frozen shards that pricked her skin. And although she jumped back to avoid the worst of it, she refused to be dissuaded, continuing to whack at the brush until she could clearly see the sky.

Unexpectedly, clearing the cave's mouth allowed easy access to the freezing wind. It whipped through her inadequate *cotte* and tore at her hair. And it stirred up the loosened debris, viciously smacking it against her feet and legs.

Forced to squeeze back inside the tunnel to avoid the wind, she leaned against the wall, considering how to proceed. Her overall sense of numbness was alarming, but she refused to entertain the jeering voice in her head that said she would freeze to death. That wasn't an option; she had to warn Nick.

Glancing down at her numb bare feet, she saw that her injured ankle was now swollen to the size of her calf. Frightened at what this might mean, she bent over, clutched her foot, and worked with trembling hands to knead life back into it.

After she'd vigorously rubbed both feet in a fruitless effort to restore circulation, she straightened and gently bounced up and down, bearing most of her weight on her healthy foot. But her feet and legs responded with as much life as two posts. And the raw air burned down her throat and into her chest. It didn't take long for her to realize she was wasting what precious little energy she had left. She sagged against the tunnel wall, too spent for tears.

And then she heard—or felt—she wasn't sure which came first—a faint vibration in the ground; the clatter of hooves. Could that be Nick riding up the trail? Or his parents? If so, she must—must—must warn them.

But in the next moment, talons of fresh terror gripped her. What if it was Jacques, coming after her? Even though a part of her knew it was an irrational fear, she could believe anything was possible after today.

Nevertheless, she knew she had to take that risk. For Nick's sake.

She forced herself to squeeze back through the slit into the cave.

Staring up at the opening, she decided only one overhanging bush looked sturdy enough to hold her weight. Raising her arms over her head, she leaped awkwardly into the air and managed to grab the slender trunk and swing her body up the side of the cave. But her momentum was insufficient; she slammed against the side of the cave, flailing wildly as she lost her grip and plunged into the snowdrift.

As she wallowed in the snow, the vibration of the approaching hoof beats grew stronger. Desperation pushed her determination to violence. She scrambled to her feet, grasped the trunk of the bush, dug in her toes, and wildly clawed her way up the side of the cave, pulling up her body with strength she didn't know she had.

Oblivious to the scratches she incurred, she tumbled through the brush and landed outside the cave, where the impact of her weight broke through the hillside's frozen snow crust. The loose snow beneath the crust swallowed her like quicksand.

Before she knew it, she was buried to her waist, trapped with the icy north wind whipping her hair around her head so harshly that the fine strands cut into the delicate skin on her face.

Gasping a shallow breath of frigid air and swallowing a surge of panic, she flopped over along the jagged edge of the snow crust, flattening her upper body across the frozen surface. Her icy fingers clutched at frozen vines sticking up through the snow, and she heaved her body out of the hole.

Panting and sweating despite the freezing temperature, she lay still for a moment as her mind shifted in and out of consciousness. But still she persisted. She had one goal, one purpose for living: She had to reach the sleigh track.

Realizing there was no way she could walk down the hill without sinking with every step, she pushed off with her hands and prayed the crust would hold her weight—like it held up under sled and sleigh runners. She swallowed her screams as she slid down the hillside on her back, scraping over brush, catching at frozen shrubs to redirect her descent.

"Uhf," was involuntarily thrust from her throat when she finally slammed into the icy berm turned up by sleigh runners. Shooting stars filled her vision, but still she clung to her purpose.

Blinking violently and sucking in labored breaths that made her chest heave, she summoned the last of her determination and slowly, inch-by-inch, dragged her aching body over the berm. "Surely they cannot miss me here," she mumbled, collapsing unconscious in the wide groove.

CHAPTER TWELVE

Nick's horse shied and reared, snorting and pawing the air, nearly unseating him. With the reins clenched tightly in one fist, Nick leaned forward and patted Chetak's neck with his free hand. He'd so enjoyed his visit with Arnold and his family that he stayed longer than he'd intended, and now he forced himself to curb his impatience.

"Whoa, boy," he soothed. "What is it?"

Pale, fading daylight filtered through the leafless tree branches and cast ominous shadowy stripes over the dark mass in the trail a short distance ahead. As Nick slid to the ground, Chetak whinnied and pawed restlessly.

Speaking softly to the skittish horse, Nick retained a firm grip on the reins while cautiously moving forward.

A body!

Chetak whinnied again, nosing Nick's arm. "It's all right, boy. Let's take a look," he soothed, patting his horse's neck.

When he reached down to turn the body face up, shock sent the blood rushing to his head; he felt faint and his heart skipped a beat. "No!"

Chetak reared, snorting fiercely. Nick pulled the reins in tight until Chetak settled, but his mind raced with questions: How did Kitty come to be this far from Burg Mosel? Where were her stockings, shoes, coat? And how did she come to look so . . . battered? Shrugging out of his heavy fur cloak, he wrapped it around her limp figure and awkwardly scooped her up in his arms.

As Nick stood there, momentarily weighing his best course of action, his parents' sleigh rounded the corner. His father hauled on the reins and slowed the sleigh to a halt.

Leaning forward simultaneously, Lord and lady Branden assessed the strange scene that appeared before them in the fading twilight. Their simultaneous gasp echoed across the crusted snow when they recognized that it was their son, minus his cloak, his tabard whipping in the wind, who stood in the sleigh track with an apparently lifeless body in his arms. Bare feet dangled from thin white legs hanging over his forearm.

"It's a child. Or a young woman," Lord Branden whispered to his wife. "Stay here. If she's still alive, she'll need your warmth."

Lord Branden jumped down from the sleigh and stomped in the track toward Nick, calling out, "What happened? Who is it?"

Nick scraped out anguished words, "It's Kitty."

"Kitty? Kitty!" Lord Branden's alarm turned to horror.

As if hearing her name, Kitty's body convulsed, startling Nick into action. He ran toward his mother carrying his precious bundle and shouting, "Quick. Make room for her."

Lady Branden jerked her hands from her ermine muff and strained to thrust aside the heavy fur blanket.

Every muscle in Nick's arms, legs, and back screamed in protest as he bent over the sleigh's side panel and deposited Kitty's lifeless body on the seat beside his mother. Lord Branden reached across his wife from the far side of the sleigh to help her tuck the blanket around Kitty's inert form. Nick released his hold on Kitty and tried to pull back, but she suddenly stirred, raising her arms and locking them around his neck in a choking grip. As she tried to speak, her teeth chattered and her words drowned in panicked sobs.

Nick hugged her to his chest, tightening his back and leg muscles to maintain his balance and clenching his stomach against the sleigh rail for support. "Relax, Kitty. I've got you. You're safe now. We'll get you home as soon as we can."

Lady Branden reached over to pry Kitty's arms from around Nick's neck, but her efforts only served to empower Kitty. She rallied, forcing out her frantic warning in a labored whisper, "Jacques tried to kill me. He put me in the secret chamber. But I found a way out. I had to warn you. He's planning to kill you."

When the three Brandens exchanged a worried glance, Kitty gripped Nick's neck tighter and tried again, more frenzied this time. "Jacques's father killed your grandmother. Jacques thinks I'm dead. And now he's planning to kill you."

Kitty's eyes closed and her body, completely spent, gave one massive shudder. Her fingers lost their tension and her arms slipped from Nick's neck. Her head fell back and her body twitched. Her head lolled sideways as her body went limp.

The three Brandens gaped at Kitty. Her words made no sense; surely, she suffered from delirium. Everyone knew Lady Rose had hidden in the secret chamber and couldn't get out. Exposure to the cold must have affected Kitty's mind.

"Is-is she . . . ?" The wind wrenched the stricken words from Nick's lips.

Lady Branden held her fingers below Kitty's nose. "No," she reassured them through fear-twisted lips, "she's still breathing. But we must get her home." She wrapped her arms around the girl and pulled her cold form against her own body to transfer heat.

* * *

Kitty stirred slightly and began mumbling incoherently. Lord Branden pushed the fur blanket under her chin until only her white forehead and coppery eyelashes resting against her scratched cheeks remained visible.

Lady Branden clutched the girl tightly. Then she tipped her head and frowned, startling her husband by demanding, "Tell me. Tell me again what she said."

"What?" Lord Branden's uncharacteristic impatience betrayed his concern for Kitty's survival.

"What did Kitty say? Tell me again," Lady Branden begged.

"Oh, just some nonsense about Jacques's father putting your mother in the secret chamber," he raised his brows, quirked his mouth, and skeptically shook his head, "and something about Jacques killing Nick." He heaved a heavy sigh and barked, "We've got to get her home."

Lady Branden's rosy, wind-bitten cheeks paled and she cried out, "Oh, dear God, help us." She began insistently shaking the bundled girl's slack body. "Wake up, Kitty. Wake up. Please. Oh, please, wake up."

Although the two men's faces registered further alarm, she ignored them. Tightening her grip, Lady Branden shook Kitty again as she questioned fiercely, "Did Jacques tell you *why* his father murdered my mother?"

Several seconds passed.

Kitty's blue-shadowed eyelids quivered.

The observers' anticipation came—and went.

Kitty didn't respond.

"Leave her be," Lord Branden growled.

But his wife ignored him. Lifting a bare hand, she administered a mild smack on Kitty's colorless cheek.

This time Kitty's pale eyelids parted a sliver. Her eyes rolled down as she tried to stabilize her gaze on the familiar face so close to her own.

Encouraged by this sign of life, Lady Branden leaned in and clearly enunciated each word, "Did you say Lady Rose was murdered by Jacques's father?"

Weak but certain came Kitty's reply. "He loved . . . Lady Rose . . . but she . . . rejected . . ." Her words trailed off as she lost consciousness again.

"Aha," Lady Branden's body stiffened, her head snapped up, and her tone held triumph, "it all makes sense now! When I stayed the winter with my father's old nurse, Edith Baer, she told me that my mother's music teacher had 'made eyes at her.'" Her gaze met her husband's. "I wasn't sure Edith's memory was clear, so I didn't ask her about it."

She frowned, explaining further, "When I asked Papa about him, he said his name was Pierre Monet— and that he must have had some great love in his life because he ignored the fawning maids." The intensity in her voice escalated, "And Jacques—his last name is

Monet, right? Jacques must be Pierre Monet's son." She caught a sharp breath. "Remember, Jacques said his father married late in life? That explains why Jacques is only a few years older than Nicky."

"But why would Pierre Monet's son—if Jacques *is* his son—come here and try to kill Kitty. Or Nick, for that matter?" Lord Branden objected.

Kitty's head lay at an awkward angle against Lady Branden's shoulder. White faced, expressionless, she appeared asleep—or worse, but at Lord Branden's protest she again roused, barely scraping out, "Revenge. Jacques's father loved Lady Rose. But she scorned him. She loved your fath . . ." her voice cracked and she sucked in air with a squeak. "Jacques expected me to marry Nick. Then if Nick were to perish and I married Jacques, everything would be his."

A tremor ran through her body and her voice faded to a mere sigh. "Believe me . . . you must believe me . . ." Kitty's eyes rolled back in her head as she lost consciousness.

* * *

"We must get Kitty out of the cold as soon as possible," Lord Branden urged. He leaped into the sleigh and grabbed the reins, calling to Nick, "We'll meet you at the back entrance."

Nick arrived first. He flung himself off Chetak and dashed to the sleigh before it came to a stop.

"Wait here while I scout around," Lord Branden instructed Nick. "I want to see if I can discover Jacques's location. There's no light in his room—I looked as we passed—so I'll check out the great room. Kitty's story sounds pretty far-fetched," he raised his brows and shrugged, "but I don't want to take any chances."

Lord Branden followed the snow-capped hedge and stopped in the garden shadows. Light shone out from the many-paned windows in the great room and reflected off the snow. Lord Branden moved in closer. Through the window he could see Jacques seated comfortably in his host's chair in front of the fire. He certainly has made himself at home, Lord Branden thought, noting the charger and goblet resting on the small table beside their guest.

Just when Lord Branden was about to turn away from the window, Jacques leaned back and pulled a small vial out of his pouch. He pinched the slender vial's top and bottom between his thumb and forefinger and lifted it up, gazing at its amber contents against the glowing backdrop of firelight. Tipping the bottle back and forth, he watched the golden liquid run from end to end. The smug expression on his face steeled Lord Branden's mind with resolve; he knew what that glass vial contained—and it wasn't a tonic or an aphrodisiac!

Straightway, Lord Branden returned to the others.

"I think Kitty was telling the truth," he confirmed gruffly then cleared his throat and gave orders, "Nick, go in quietly. Find Josef and send him out; he can carry Kitty. Rosamund, you go in with Josef and take Kitty to your sitting room. When you're safely in, Nick and I will go to the great room. We'll pour up some mead and visit with Jacques. That will buy you some time. Get Kitty settled and then come down in a panic and tell us that she isn't in her room—which will be the truth. At that point, we can question Jacques to see if he admits knowing what happened to her. We'll go from there."

He turned to Nick. "Get the dungeon key from the clerk's office; it's still in its old hiding place. I expect we'll need it," he concluded grimly, then added, "I'll stay here until Josef comes out. You wait for me in my clerk's office."

Nick sped silently out of the stable to do his father's bidding.

* * *

Jacques, his eyes half closed, stared into the fire. His thin hands moved back and forth along Lord Branden's chair arms as he settled back in satisfaction. He was here. At Burg Mosel. At last.

As he curled his thin fingers over the paws carved into the ends of the chair arms and rested his head against the lion's head carved into the chair back, his thoughts returned to his childhood. His over-worked mother had been too busy trying to make ends meet by working two jobs to give him much-needed attention. At best, his clothes had been shabby and food inadequate. Life had never been happy and carefree. Even in his youth, work had provided a rewarding escape from the never-ending disappointments of home, and for years it had filled his whole life.

He recalled his father. A man who could make music with two sticks. A man who drank too much. A man given to fits of rage. And when Pierre Monet died in a drunken fight over a paltry sum of money owed to him, a sad peace settled over the household.

When his father's few belongings were dispersed, Jacques received a small metal box containing his father's diary. Initially, he'd shoved it under his bed, disdaining it for its lack of monetary value, but on the first anniversary of his father's death, he'd retrieved it and spent an afternoon getting acquainted with the man his father had once been.

Included in the record was an account of his father's year at Burg Mosel. It was all there: his father's passion for Lady Rose, her disdainful rejection, his father's ultimate revenge.

Discovering the reason behind his father's drunkenness and abuse drove Jacques's anger at his father into a bitter obsession. Indeed, in his twisted thinking, Lady Rose had gotten what she deserved. After all, not only had she scorned his father's love, she'd thwarted his own destiny. Had she returned his father's love, *he* would have been her son and heir.

A diabolical plot took shape in Jacques's sick mind, a scheme to acquire what he deemed his deserved inheritance. For the past three years he'd been preparing for this day, meticulously working out the details with painstaking care.

He'd learned about the Branden family through the unwitting chatter of a musician friend who'd been a guest at Burg Mosel. He knew they had a ward, Kitty. He knew Nick was the Branden's only surviving child. He knew when Nick departed for Charles University. And he knew precisely when Nick was to journey home. He'd deliberately encountered Nick, intending to strike up a friendship, or better yet, wangle an invitation to Burg Mosel. That invitation had required no overt effort; Nick was as unsuspecting as a schoolboy. Surely, the ease of the connection proved the justice of his cause.

And what he'd anticipated being the biggest obstacle—convincing Nick and Kitty to marry—proved to be no obstacle at all. Even if they weren't aware of it, it was obvious they were already in love with each other; he'd only needed to stimulate a bit of jealousy.

But somehow his plan went awry. How could he know Kitty would leave her room this afternoon? After all, her accident had seemed to indicate that fate was on his side. And he'd *needed* the wine; he'd

Joyce Williams

gone without enough to satisfy his thirst for over a week. But this afternoon there'd been plenty of time and the privacy to allow him to indulge his craving.

Certainly it wasn't *his* fault that Kitty had overheard him. What was she doing, eavesdropping in that suit of armor? He should thank his lucky stars that she'd sneezed and exposed her treachery. Really, she'd left him no alternative. He now understood his father's revenge. With deliberate precision, he'd re-enacted the scenario described in his father's diary and left his victim to die in the secret chamber.

It was, after all, perhaps for the best. Kitty was beautiful—no one would deny that. But she was also strong-minded. And who wanted that quality in a wife? No, this was surely fate dealing him the winning hand.

He lifted his right hand from its resting place on the chair arm and reached his long fingers into his pouch as smug satisfaction settled over his thin face. Retrieving the small vial of liquid poison, he held it up to the firelight and rolled it over and over between his fingers. It promised his plan's success and the fulfillment of his destiny: when the family assembled to discuss Kitty's disappearance, he would thoughtfully suggest a little wine would calm their tension. He smirked; he'd had the foresight to suggest the maid should refill the wine decanter he'd emptied earlier. And slipping this vial's golden contents into the wine would take care of everything else. He'd avenge his father's rejection—and he'd have revenge for the abuse he'd suffered. With the Brandens out of the way, he could step in and bring order to the chaos that would surely result. It was all really very simple.

Jacques continued to manipulate the vial, repeatedly tipping it one way and then the other, then rolling it over and over between his fingers. He smiled, watching the amber liquid glide smoothly up and down, back and forth. It was mesmerizing, that golden solution.

As he stared at it, he imagined himself as lord of the Branden's vast estate. He could even take their name—that would be the ultimate revenge. He leaned his head back and closed his eyes.

Footsteps thudded in the corridor. Alarmed by reality's intrusion into his fantasy, Jacques jumped up from Lord Branden's chair and hastily shoved the vial into his pouch before Lord Branden and Nick entered the great room. His calm expression belied the excitement surging through his blood; today the stars were aligned in his favor.

CHAPTER THIRTEEN

Nick carefully eased open the back door to minimize its creaking and tiptoed inside just as Josef emerged from the scullery stairwell. Seeing Nick, Josef's face broke into a broad smile, but before he could speak Nick put his finger to his lips, signaling silence.

Nick repeated Lord Branden's instructions while Josef listened intently. Offering Nick a brief nod, the older man departed through the door Nick had just entered.

Nick didn't bother to light a candle in the clerk's office; he knew his way around the room, even in the dark. Raising a corner of the heavy hunt-scene tapestry that covered most of one wall, he reached into the small hole in the wall behind it, his fingers tightening around the thick brass key hidden there. He threaded one of the laces at the neck of his tabard through the hole in the bow of the key and then quickly dropped it inside the fabric against his skin, where it could remain out of sight but easily accessible. He leaned against the door frame and closed his eyes, waiting for his father.

"It's me, Son," his father's whisper near his ear startled Nick; he jumped and swallowed his gasp.

They stood together in the dark, watching through the doorway as Lady Branden came in, followed by Josef carrying Kitty's limp form. His father's arm dropped across his shoulders and tightened reassuringly. Nick felt his tension ease a bit as the little procession tiptoed up the stairs; even Josef, whose footsteps normally thumped, managed to move noiselessly.

When sufficient time had passed for Lady Branden to settle Kitty, Lord Branden tapped Nick's arm in a silent signal; it was time to move. As they walked along the corridor toward the great room, Lord Branden loudly recounted the details of their visit with Letty and her granddaughter.

"So, you're back," Jacques observed when Lord Branden and Nick entered the room.

Before either one had time to answer, rapid footsteps could be heard pounding along the corridor toward the great room. Lord Branden turned his head toward the door, his stolid face giving no indication of concern or anticipation.

Nick's emotions churned like a seething cauldron in his stomach. Worry about Kitty's condition and suspicion of Jacques's duplicity tightened his chest and throat muscles, leaving him dry-mouthed and short of breath, but he felt a swelling of admiration for his father's composure. He sensed that the next few moments would set in motion events that would forever alter life at Burg Mosel. Oh, to be able to retract his impulsive invitation to Jacques.

He shook himself mentally; now was not the time to berate himself over regrets.

Lady Branden dashed into the room. She looked genuinely frantic—too genuine for Nick's peace of mind. He had never seen his mother lose her dignity, but wide-eyed and red-faced, she was so convincing he never would have guessed she was pretending if he hadn't been a party to the plan.

"Kitty's not in her room. I can't find her—anywhere . . ." When his mother's feverish exclamation ended in a wail, Nick's heart leapt with pride. What an incredible lady, his mother.

Seizing her husband's arm, Lady Branden tugged impatiently. Her crazed eyes and shallow, wheezing breaths made Nick almost believe that Kitty truly was missing. "Oh, Erik, where could she have gone?" she demanded in a high-pitched voice. "Maybe she bumped her head when she fell off Bohdan and I just didn't realize it; what if she's disoriented and wandered outside? We've got to find her."

Lord Branden circled his arm around his wife and pressed her face against his chest, as if he expected his strength would enable her to regain control of her nerves. His words were low and reassuring. "Steady now, Rosamund. No need to be alarmed. With her injured ankle, I'm sure Kitty couldn't have gone far. Did you check with Nora?"

"Yes. But Nora hasn't seen her since we left earlier today." Her tone escalated again, "And I even had Josef check the south wing—including the storage room."

"This is a big place, my dear. I'm sure we'll find her."

He turned his attention to Jacques, addressing him in a normal voice over his wife's head. "Jacques, did you see Kitty this afternoon?"

Nick was so caught up in the drama of the moment that he nearly forgot that Kitty was safely ensconced in his mother's suite. With effort he kept his mouth from gaping at his father's slow tact.

"No, I didn't see her," Jacques replied soberly. "I've been sitting here by the fire, soaking up the heat ever since I returned from riding. Matilda kindly brought me a tray a little while ago," he gestured toward the goblet and charger on the side table. Cocking his head in a puzzled manner, he added, "I assumed Kitty was in her room, resting her injured foot."

Jacques's glance settled on Lady Branden's trembling form still clinging to her husband's solid frame. When he moved confidently toward the sideboard, Nick gulped, knowing that Matilda would have refilled the decanters when she delivered the tray. And when Jacques offered solicitously, "Perhaps a little wine would strengthen Lady Branden," Nick broke out in a cold sweat. What if something went wrong? But his anxiety was short-lived.

He'd never seen his father move so fast. Before Nick could even blink, Lord Branden clamped a hard hand on Jacques's shoulder and spun him around.

"Wait one minute, young man."

Quickly capitalizing on his stunned surprise, Jacques's tone oozed indulgence. "Why, Lord Branden, I only meant to be helpful. We're all a bit distraught just now." He raised his brows and smiled benevolently. "Even you, my lord."

"And with good reason," Lord Branden stated firmly, herding Jacques back into his chair. "This situation has gone far enough." He gave a sharp tug on the nearby bell cord as he glanced at his wife and son. "Sit down, both of you," he said before turning toward the entrance as Matilda, who'd obviously heard them arrive, appeared in the doorway.

"Inform the household staff they are to report to me here. Immediately!"

Lord Branden's bark was so out of character that Matilda stuttered. "Y-yes, my lord." She didn't question her master's orders, but her bulging eyes betrayed her shock. She bobbed a brief curtsy and fled.

Lord Branden offered no pleasant conversation and no one uttered a single word. Ever the quiet, genial gentleman, he had abruptly emerged as Lord of the Manor.

Jacques folded his hands in his lap and leaned back, wearing a complacent expression on his face.

Lady Branden covered her mouth with shaking fingers and stared at the floor.

Nick looked around, wondering what his father would do next.

The servants began to arrive, each one falling silent when they saw the sober faces of those already in the room. When all were present, Lord Branden ordered the staff to form a single line in front of the windows—all except Josef; Lord Branden stationed him in the doorway like a sentinel. Then slowly, deliberately, his body held stiffly erect, Lord Branden strode to the fireplace. Everyone's eyes followed him but no one moved. Taking up a fire iron, Lord Branden stabbed the flames into a rousing blaze. When he finally turned around, the hard expression on his face and the cold steel in his blue eyes sent fear rippling across the servants' faces.

Nick felt the muscle twitch in his cheek—he'd never seen his father so angry.

"I've called you here to witness what I'm going to say." His eyes traveled from face to face. They stopped at Jacques.

Brittle intensity strained his voice. "This young man," he gestured toward their guest, "Jacques Monet, is the son of Pierre Monet, the music instructor for my wife's mother when she was a young woman. As you all know, Lady Rose disappeared here at Burg Mosel during her husband's cousin's wedding festivities, and no one knew her fate until many years later. My wife grew up without a mother, and her father, Lord Schmidden, lost his wife and their expected second child."

Lord Branden's piercing eyes surveyed his subjects, who remained as motionless as a still life captured on an artist's canvas when he addressed them. "Today, our very own Kitty overheard this man, Jacques Monet," he gestured toward their guest, "boasting in this very room that his father had deliberately trapped Lady Rose in the secret chamber."

Wide-eyed, the servants watched Lord Branden, but the silence in the room was as heavy with portent as the silence between thunder claps.

"And would you like to know why?" Lord Branden seemed to be deliberately drawing out the suspense—it was so tangible that Nick could almost smell it. He stole a quick glance at Jacques, noting that his guest's face remained expressionless.

Lord Branden answered his own question. "Because she rejected his inappropriate behavior, choosing instead to remain faithful to her husband."

A few stifled gasps punctuated the servants' shock.

Then, in a single moment, Jacques became the focus of fourteen pairs of eyes. He raised one sandy brow, shook his head, and scorned, "What a preposterous story!"

"Is it, now?" Lord Branden's tone was deceptively mild. "When we returned home this evening, we found Kitty nearly frozen to death in a sleigh track far down the hillside?" He raised the fire iron and pointed it at their guest. "Explain that."

Nick saw Jacques's pupil's dilate and his hands tighten on the chair arms; the noose he'd spread for others had closed in on him.

Lord Branden lowered his arm and pounded the fire iron on the stone floor as his gaze swept over the servants' faces. "Would you like to hear Kitty's story?"

Like one giant heart-beat, the servants leaned toward their master. Kitty was a favorite, and a threat to her was a threat to them—and to the family who provided their livelihood.

"When Jacques discovered that Kitty had overheard his plan to poison Nick, he choked her." Lord Branden pounded the floor again and cinched the noose cord tight, "The bruises on her neck bear witness to her account."

Jacques's breath, drawn in like a hiss, was followed by a curse. "Mon Dieu!" he exclaimed, vaulting to his feet, "I am being framed."

A chorus of outraged servants' voices formed a descant to the impassioned words that exploded from Lady Branden's lips as she sprang out of her chair. "What do you mean, you're being framed? Your father *murdered* my mother," her blazing eyes stared out from her pale face and her whole body shook, "and *you* tried to kill our Kitty."

"Sit down, both of you. I am not finished," Lord Branden did not raise his voice, but its force was almost a visible thing. He pounded the fire iron on the stone floor again, a call to order.

Ramrod stiff, Jacques sank back down in his seat, his lower lip curled with the injured air of someone unjustly victimized.

Lady Branden sagged against the arm of her chair. With tightened jaw and clenched teeth she sniffed sharply while squeezing one hand around the other in a knuckle-whitening grip. Nick knew that this time her distress was not play-acting. His heart throbbed fiercely in his throat. How would it all end?

Lord Branden continued, "When Jacques discovered that Kitty had overheard his plan, he decided to get rid of her," his jaw tightened as he growled, "and he nearly succeeded. He followed his father's example, locking her in the secret chamber. However, brave and clever girl that she is, Kitty escaped. Without stockings, shoes, or cloak, she risked her life to intercept us on our way home so she could warn us of his diabolical plan."

Jacques sat very still. His thin fingers tensed spasmodically on his chair arms, and his eyes burned like two black spots in his head. Nick saw him eyeing the servants, but any hope for sympathy from them was now gone. He was the object of their disgust; their faces said so.

As Lord Branden's intent gaze travelled slowly around the room, his eyes met each pair looking back at him before he reassured them, "Kitty is now safe."

His focus settled on Jacques and his words came out in a roar, "And *you* are no longer a guest at Burg Mosel."

Unconsciously, the staff, in one movement, took a menacing step toward Jacques.

Lord Branden's attention remained fixed on Jacques as he held out his hand to Nick, "The key to the dungeon."

"Right here, Father." Nick snagged the key from its hiding place inside his tabard.

Before Lord Branden could reach out to take it, Jacques's right hand, subtly creeping toward his pouch, caught his attention. In the next instant, Lord Branden's large, sinewy hands manacled Jacques's forearms and in one swift motion he jerked them high above his head.

"Josef, your assistance, please."

The request was a command, and Josef stood beside him before the words had hardly passed his lips. Moving together in one rapid motion, the two men hauled Jacques out of his chair.

"Nick, remove his pouch," his father's terse command brought Nick to his feet. "Take out the vial of poison he planned to add to our drinks."

The staff's faces mirrored their shock.

Staring at Jacques's belly to avoid his eyes, Nick untied the pouch's leather cords. He suppressed a shiver; it was hard to be so close to him, knowing he'd faked friendship and then tried to kill Kitty. Nick slid the small bag onto the nearby table and quickly loosened the drawstrings. As he extracted the amber vial, his father's sharp command interrupted his thoughts.

"Empty it into the fire, Son."

Nick lifted his head. With a quick twist, he uncorked the small bottle. Then he swung around and pitched the contents into the fire. A loud whoosh was followed by a brief sizzle. He quickly tossed the empty vial into the fire to evaporate any residue left on the glass.

"Go down ahead of us and unlock the door to the dungeon," Lord Branden directed Nick as he and Josef maneuvered their prisoner toward the corridor. As they neared the door he turned back to address the wide-eyed servants, "Staff dismissed."

Lenka rushed straight to her mistress, her face flushed and eyes wide with anxiety. "Oh, my lady, is Miss Kitty all right?"

"Come with me. We'll go check on her." Lady Branden's voice trembled, but Nick noted with relief that color had returned to her cheeks.

CHAPTER FOURTEEN

"Your father murdered my mother!" His mother's impassioned cry played over and over in Nick's mind as he sat beside his father in the large family sleigh, *en route* to deliver their prisoner to Nuremberg for justice. They had been traveling for over eight hours today and anticipated reaching their destination before dark.

Jacques sat on the wooden seat behind Nick, heavy leather cords binding his wrists and ankles. A traveling chest and Jacques's trunk filled the space beside Jacques.

Overnight, the weather had turned viciously cold. A shudder rippled through his father's large frame, prompting Nick to offer, "I'll take the reins, Father. Put your hands under the furs so they'll get warm."

As Lord Branden handed Nick the reins, he said

faintly, "Thanks, Son. My left arm pains me fiercely. I don't want to worry you, but . . ."

Following that brief mention of his discomfort, Lord Branden wheezed a constricted breath and suddenly shot up from his seat, clawing violently at his chest as he tried to breath.

Startled, Nick extended his legs and stood up, employing his full body weight to jerk on the reins. The horses screamed and plowed through the snow as the sleigh jolted to a rough halt. Nick turned to his father.

But it was too late. His father was slumped sideways on the seat and his skin had taken on a gray pallor.

Intent on his father's condition, Nick missed the black triumph suffusing Jacques's face as he lifted high his shackled arms and slammed them down against the back of Nick's neck, knocking him unconscious. Using his bound arms like a lever, Jacques ruthlessly propelled Nick's limp body out of the sleigh into the snow.

The crash and ensuing thud spooked the horses. They leaped ahead, throwing Jacques out of the sleigh. He landed head-first in the snow.

The team bolted, dragging the sleigh that tipped crazily from side to side. Jacques's trunk bounced out of the sleigh and burst open upon impact, its contents spewing out over the snow.

* * *

Dazed but unhurt, Jacques rolled over, bent his knees, and sat up. He blew the snow from his nostrils and scraped his manacled arms over his snow-frosted face. Blinking vigorously against the glaring sheen of the snow, he looked around. Movement in the distance caught his eye; the run-away team and sleigh were now a rapidly disappearing speck.

Cursing angrily under his breath, he muttered, "Fool horses." He would have to walk the rest of the way.

Determined to cut himself free, Jacques lay back down in the snow and rolled over and over until he bumped Nick's inert form.

He snorted again to clear his nose and then scoured his face with his sleeve. By thrashing in the snow, he jockeyed his body so his fingers could reach the knife he knew Nick carried in a sheath at his waist. It took several attempts, but Jacques finally worked the knife out of the sheath.

Pointing the sharp blade away from his body, Jacques rolled onto his back and pulled his knees to his chest. With short sawing strokes, he cut through the leather straps binding his ankles. Scrambling to his feet, he squatted with the knife clamped between his boots and sawed at the cords binding his wrists.

When his hands broke free, he pounced on his broken, half-buried chest. Holding the knife in one hand, he used the other to scrape away the snow. The drawer sprang open when he pressed the button. He retrieved the metal box containing his father's diary and shoved it inside the neck of his clothing.

Casting a brief glance at Nick's motionless body, Jacques's eyes narrowed shrewdly on the bulging coin pouch tied at his waist. As Jacques slashed the ties and snagged the pouch, Nick groaned. Startled, Jacques clamped the pouch under his arm and swung the knife in the air.

Nick opened his eyes in time to see Jacques's fist, raised with the knife point directed at his throat. A rush of fear gave him strength; his arm came up and he caught Jacques's wrist in time to deflect the strike.

Jacques fell sideways, losing his grip on the weapon. Nick's hand closed around the knife handle, and despite the intense pain in his neck and head, he raised up and swung the knife at his attacker.

Suddenly defenseless, Jacques scrambled away from Nick, leaped to his feet, and escaped on foot, cursing loudly with every step.

Nick watched Jacques until the pain in his head took over. With a low moan, he sank back into the snow.

* * *

After an hour of wandering, dragging the sleigh that had miraculously remained upright on its runners, the team of horses came full circle. One of them nudged Nick's feet. When Nick didn't respond, she whinnied softly and nuzzled his head.

Nick came to, choking on the earthy, oat smell of moist horse breath. "Uuuggghhh," he sputtered, raising his gloved hand to push away the horse's head, only to discover that he was still gripping his knife. When he groaned, the horse nudged him again.

"All right, old girl." Nick slid his knife back into its sheath then rolled onto his side and sat up. He reached up stiff fingers to knead the throbbing muscles in the back of his neck while he searched the horizon for any sign of Jacques. All that met his eyes was a sea of white, but a quick scan of the snow-blanketed meadow revealed Jacques's footprints punched in the white crust and leading toward a stand of linden trees, marking his escape route.

Heavy with an icy coating of melted-then-frozen moisture, his fur-lined winter clothing hampered his progress as he trudged laboriously toward the sleigh, although it had undoubtedly prevented him freezing to death.

"Thank you, God," he whispered fervently, grateful to be alive and that the renegade horses had come back to him.

As he approached the sleigh, one of his father's boots sticking out at an unnatural angle made his breath freeze in his lungs. And when he leaned into the sleigh, the blue eyes staring vacantly back at him confirmed his fears and told their tragic tale. He gently closed his father's eyelids, unprepared for the pain that exploded in his chest and threatened to suffocate him. He dropped his head to the sleigh rail, unable to move.

His father was dead.

Jacques had escaped.

And he was still miles from Nuremberg.

Finally, stiff from the cold, heavy-limbed and heavy hearted, Nick choked back his grief. He clenched his fists and gritted his teeth. He had no choice; he had to keep going.

As he heaved his body into the sleigh, he tossed an irritated glance at Jacques's broken trunk and scattered belongings but decided he felt no responsibility to salvage any of it.

By sheer grit, he succeeded in raising his father's body into a sitting position on the bench. Then, exhausted and clammy with perspiration, he dropped down and scooted in beside the body to catch his wind and consider his situation.

He readily recognized the need for haste: the sun had dropped out of sight, an easterly wind was blowing and picking up force, and thick gray clouds were quickly moving in to blot out what light remained. The world seemed as bleak as his heart.

Shivering as he looked around for their fur blankets, he heard them flapping in the wind before he saw them. They had tumbled into the snow and were caught under Jacques's broken trunk, and their loose corners snapped like thunderclaps as they hit the frozen snow crust. Nick clenched his jaw, forced his arms and legs to obey his will, and clambered out of the sleigh to collect them.

Deciding it would be best to appear as normal as possible, he struggled to tuck one of the blankets around his father's body before wrapping himself in the second one and collapsing to the seat. He sat there for a moment, shaking with cold and shock. Inside his fur-lined gloves, his fingers were numb, and he dropped the reins twice before successfully securing them in his stiff fist.

Finally, in response to his feeble command, the team pulled ahead.

CHAPTER FIFTEEN

The wind picked up as twilight settled over the tree-dotted countryside. Nick riveted his eyes on the dim outline of chimney smoke rising into the sky above the rolling hills, hoping his assumption that it marked his destination was correct and that he would arrive before it grew so dark he couldn't find his way.

Several hours later, when he felt confident he'd sighted the Nuremberg Castle towers against the horizon, the tension in his stomach finally eased. But as he got closer, the wind grew violent and snow started to fall, big, thick flakes of it. The towers appeared and disappeared in a swirling white shroud, forcing him to squint. By the time he crossed the bridge spanning the Pegnitz River that provided entrance to the city, all he could think about was finding a bed.

Nick squinted through ice-crusted eyelashes to make out the guild signs and building names as his sleigh runners skidded wildly over the icy, narrow, cobbled streets boxed between ghostly buildings. At last he pulled up to the door of an inn, relieved that there was a nearby stable. He straightened his stiff limbs and gripped the sleigh rail for balance as he jumped out.

But the frosty ground was deceptively slick.

Nick's feet flew out from under him. The reins whizzed through his hand. The rail jammed into his armpit. And he clung to the sleigh, gasping and shaking, vastly relieved that his horses hadn't spooked.

When he'd caught his breath and regained his balance, he grimaced—and flinched. His arm and ribs ached and his lower lip stung like fire. He dabbed his mouth with his gloved hand. It came away stained with a dark, wet smear. Blood.

Sucking his lower lip into his mouth, he pressed it between his teeth and ran his tongue over the split in the tender skin. Nausea roiled in his empty stomach, and he suddenly felt light-headed. He doubled over, clutching the rail for support.

When the world finally stopped spinning, Nick collected the reins and tied them securely to a snow-capped hitching post. As he stumbled toward the low, snow-crusted wooden door under the frosted sign, House of the Copper Pig, swirling haze carried in a gust of wind blinded him, but the faint buzz of voices coming from within served as a guide.

His numb fingers fumbled with the latch, but he finally managed to open the door. When he staggered inside, the warm air stung his cheeks and chin, and the strong, yeasty smell of fermented hops hung in the air. As he shoved the door closed and turned into the dimly-lit room, tears collected in the corners of his eyes.

He leaned against the closed door and finally managed to focus on a wizened old man with a scrubby beard and broken-toothed grin, who was bantering with several patrons from his post behind the counter that flanked the side wall.

The old man interrupted his conversation, "What can I do ya fer, Stranger? Need yer liver warmed?" His barrel belly shook with his jovial laugh as he gestured with his fist, first toward the keg and then to the shelf behind him, where assorted bottles ranging from pale amber to bright burgundy awaited his choice. Cocking his head and lifting a questioning eyebrow, the rotund fellow slammed a lidded tankard down on the counter.

Nick waved his hand, dismissing the offer. He deliberately ignored the curious stares of the room's occupants—he saw at a glance that a dozen or so men were gathered around tables and playing pochspiel, a bluffing card game.

"A room and stable space for the night," Nick said tersely as he eyed the nearby stairs leading to the second floor, "and a stable boy to assist me with my horses."

The proprietor's leathery face brightened at the prospect of a paying, overnight guest. He beckoned to a raggedly-clad youth frisking with a mangy pup near the fireplace, calling, "Bert, help the gent'man."

The lad jumped up eagerly. "This 'ere way, my lord," he invited, peering through uncombed brown hair with bright, hungry eyes. A big boy, Bert was sturdy and overgrown for his clothes.

Nick's heart dropped to his boots when he reached for the gold coins to pay for his requested services. His pouch was missing! Could it have come loose when Jacques knocked him out of the sleigh? Or in the scuffle when Jacques had attacked him? He threw up a silent prayer that his father's pouch was still with his body and not also lost somewhere in the snow-covered meadow.

"I'll be back to pay you when I'm settled," Nick promised the old man before he followed Bert into the snowstorm. As the door closed, he heard the patrons resume their conversations.

"Is there a carpenter nearby, someone who builds coffins?" Nick questioned Bert in a low voice as soon as they were alone. "My father died on our way here, so I need to take care of his body immediately."

"Yes, my lord. In the next block, just. You want I should go fer ya?" Bert volunteered.

"Please. And whatever casket they have on hand will be fine. The simpler, the better."

Bert nodded his head vigorously and pounded on the nearby stable door to give notice of the newly arrived guest before he disappeared around the corner.

The stable door opened and the lantern's light shone out like a beacon. Nick quickly drove his team and sleigh inside. Relieved to get the horses to shelter, he made the effort to smile at the scrawny lad who uncoupled the horses from the sleigh and led them to a trough of oats and a tank of fresh water.

Anticipating Bert's imminent return, Nick climbed into the sleigh and anxiously pushed aside the fur blanket and heavy fur coat encasing his father's body. At first glance, he could see that his father's pouch was not in its usual location covering his stomach. A wave of panic shot through him: What if he had no money? But in the next moment, he released a deep sigh; his father's pouch, heavy with gold coins, had slid around his waist and was safe, hidden under his tabard.

Nick wiped his sweat-beaded face against his sleeve, then he stripped off his gloves and tried to loosen the knot securing the pouch. It took several tries with his cold-stiffened fingers before he managed to tug open the neck.

He fished out several gold coins, which he clamped between his teeth while he fastened the pouch around his own waist and then slid its considerable bulk under his tabard—there was no need to advertise his resources and make himself a target for theft.

Within a few minutes, Bert returned, trailed by two burly men shouldering a long, wooden box. Giving Nick their promise to keep Lord Branden's body in the Death House until he came to claim it, the men efficiently lifted his father's body and laid it in the coffin.

When the hinged lid banged shut, Nick cringed, and in that instant, he resolved to bring Jacques to justice. His father's death had thrust upon him a monstrous responsibility. Murder and death threats, challenges to his family, to the girl he loved, to his own life—and now his father's death would not, indeed, could not, go unanswered.

Shouldering two heavy fur blankets, Nick accompanied Bert the short distance along the half-timber and stone wall that connected the stable to the inn. Just before they reached the door, he slipped the boy a gold coin for his services, certain it couldn't hurt to have a friend in this strange place.

He stopped at the counter, paid his bill, and quietly climbed the stairs to the first room at the top.

The room was cold, and Nick shivered as he struggled to remove his heavy boots from feet that had lost all feeling hours ago. He peeled off his outer clothing and hung the disheveled garments on the three convenient pegs sticking out of the wall near the door. Yes, his body ached all over. But worse, his heart felt numb. He wrapped himself in his fur blankets and stretched out on the straw-filled tick.

But sleep, though he wished for it desperately, refused to come. His feet gradually thawed, stinging as the nerves regained sensation, while his mind traced and retraced the events of the day now past.

Shortly before dawn, physical exhaustion overtook him, and he finally slept.

* * *

The milk wagon's metal rimmed wheels rattled over the cobbles in the narrow street in front of the inn, and the enticing aroma of baking bread wafted up from below. Nick's stomach growled, waking him with a start, reminding him that he'd eaten nothing since yesterday morning. He ran his tongue over his lower lip and winced when it met the crusted scab. He threw off the furs, jerked on his clothing, and tugged on his boots. Painful memories flooded his mind. He scraped his hand over his whisker-stubbled face in a familial gesture of trying to erase unwanted thoughts and hardened himself against his emotions.

It would do no good to fixate on his sorrow; the task before him would require all his wits.

The innkeeper's plump, cheerful wife called to him as he descended the stairs, his furs hoisted over one shoulder. "You're a sleepin' one, and that's for certain." She beamed a toothy grin at him as she grabbed a ladle and an earthenware bowl. "Be wanting a bite to eat, now would ya?" She plopped the bowl filled with steaming porridge beside a tin pitcher of top milk on the long oak table near him.

Nick dumped his furs on the bench, seated himself at the table, and poured the thick cream over his porridge. He gave it a stir and began to eat. Not really listening to the woman's ramblings, his mind raced over the plans he'd made in the night. But her words suddenly penetrated his thoughts.

". . . nigh to frozen, he was. Said his horse threw him and ran off. My good husband, he's what just now's givin' him a lift to Doc Graber's. I'm awonderin' how he's to be gettin' on. His feet and hands . . . my, my . . ." she mused, shaking her gray head.

Nick lowered his spoon.

Unaware of Nick's reaction, the woman resumed her chatter. "Name of Jacques, that's what he said.

A gent'man he 'ppeared to be, what with his fine clothes and gold coins."

Nick leaped to his feet. So! His pouch hadn't fallen into the snow. Jacques had stolen it!

In one fluid motion he scooped up his furs and strode out the door, his rash departure leaving the garrulous woman staring after him with her mouth open, her words dangling mid-sentence.

Young Bert, obviously waiting for Nick to make an appearance, darted toward him when he bolted into the street. "At yer service, my lord."

"My team and sleigh," Nick growled, ignoring the clear sky and the sun sparkling off the surrounding snow-covered rooftops.

Taking no notice of Nick's gruffness, Bert dashed away to do his bidding.

When Bert returned leading the horses and sleigh, Nick dumped the furs in the back and climbed in, reaching for the reins. "Direct me to the nearest magistrate," he barked, his frown deepening as his teeth worried the scab on his lip.

Bert took the request as an invitation. He jumped into the sleigh beside Nick and pointed to the left. "This 'ere way, my lord."

CHAPTER SIXTEEN

Nick bent his long legs and dropped to the edge of a straight-backed chair in Johann Wolf's small, unheated office. The mingled smells of old leather and stale beer filled his nostrils. Magistrate Wolf's wood heeled boots clicked loudly in the silence, and Nick noted the dulled patina in the oak floor's traffic areas. Light from the one small window highlighted the ink splotches staining the desk top. One wall featured columns of built-in drawers. Several mismatched wood chairs and a table holding an oil lantern completed the room's furnishings.

Responding to the magistrate's inquiry, Nick outlined the events of the previous three weeks. Striving to present an appeal dominated with facts rather than emotions, he nevertheless had difficulty keeping his voice steady when he mentioned Jacques attempts to murder Kitty and then him.

The magistrate eyed him shrewdly and emitted a short "Humph" when Nick described Kitty's desperate effort to warn him.

Nick ended his report with the innkeeper's wife's statement that Jacques was seeking medical care from Dr. Graber. The magistrate scowled, his piercing eyes burrowing beneath his heavy brows while he considered the appropriate course of action.

"Let me see if I've got your story straight. A man named Jacques Monet threatened you and attempted to murder your parents' ward?"

Nick felt the magistrate's assessing gaze. He knew his clothing supported his title and his articulate speech confirmed an aristocratic education, nevertheless, he felt awkward stating his name as Lord Branden. Of course, that title now belonged to him and he would certainly use it to his advantage, but he knew it carried with it not only respect and honor but also a solemn duty to protect those under his jurisdiction.

Raising his chin decisively, Magistrate Wolf rose to his feet. "We'll visit Dr. Graber."

"Is it far? You can ride with me," Nick offered, leading the way to his sleigh where Bert waited.

Magistrate Wolf directed them through several narrow streets and narrower-still alleys, until they emerged into the town square that centered on the Schoner Brunnen, the fountain holding pride of place in Nuremberg's central square. The three-tiered pyramid soared up from an octagonal water basin, featured forty sculptures including Moses and seven Biblical prophets, and ended in a cruciform finial that resembled a cathedral spire. And to everyone giving a 360-degree twist to the brass ring attached on the fountain's southwest side, legend promised good luck.

Nick eyed the fountain and then glanced around the square. *Panienkirche*, the Church of Our Lady, bordered the east side and drew his attention. Above the richly decorated porch, the Mannleinlaufen, a clock with mechanical figures that paced around the statue of Emperor Charles IV every day at noon, told the time. It was nine-fifteen.

His gaze moved to Das Rathouse, the town hall dominating the square's north side and harboring in its bowels dungeon cells and torture instruments for punishing criminals.

His quick glance up at Luginsland and Sinwell

Towers, rising above Nuremberg Castle from the sandstone cliff overshadowing the city, was redirected by the magistrate, who guided them around the fountain and pointed to a street on the right leading away from the square. They took the turn and made several more before finally arriving on Egidienplatz.

"There 'tis," Bert said eagerly, pointing down the street to a whitewashed lathe and plaster house rising from a stone foundation. Displaying two serpents twined around a staff, a physician's guild sign hung above the door and swayed in the slight breeze.

As Nick reined the team to a stop, Magistrate Wolf jumped down, bounded up to the entrance, and rapped sharply.

When a portly, white-bearded man opened the door and peered out, Magistrate Wolf inquired, "Dr. Graber?" At the doctor's nod, he wasted no words, "Johann Wolf. Magistrate."

Nick observed the two men sizing up each other. "At your service," the doctor replied, executing a slight bow.

Nick could hear loud groans coming through the

open doorway. The doctor hastily stepped outside and pulled the door shut, but his attempt to hide the disturbing sounds failed. Nick recognized Jacques's voice cursing the pain, and he struggled not to rejoice at his tormentor's suffering.

"We want to question you about a man whom Lord Branden," Magistrate Wolf gestured toward Nick waiting in the sleigh, "states threatened his life and attempted to murder his parents' ward. We understand this man suffers from frost-bite and is presently in your care."

"Can Lord Branden identify the man you seek?" The magistrate beckoned to Nick, who tossed the reins to Bert and jumped out of the sleigh. As he walked up to the door, the groans coming from inside the house grew louder.

When the doctor peered intently at Nick from below bushy white eyebrows, Nick met his scrutiny with a steady glance.

Magistrate Wolf instructed, "Describe the man you're looking for."

"He's tall and thin, has cropped brown hair and brown eyes. His face is narrow. He has a sharp nose and pointed chin. His fingers are long and thin, and he wears a small gold ring displaying two clasped hands on his left pinkie finger. He has a pouch full of gold coins that he stole from me, and that's his voice I hear coming from inside your house."

Dr. Graber's brow furrowed as Nick described Jacques, and when Nick was finished, he said, "You certainly described my patient. He's here, and he won't be going anywhere for quite some time. His fingers and toes are gravely frostbitten; in fact, he may lose some of them. His right foot is particularly bad, and I fear I shall have to amputate it." He turned and opened the door, ushering them inside.

As Nick's eyes adjusted to the dimly lit room, his gaze gravitated to Jacques, reclining on a pine settle. His bandaged feet were propped on top of three pillows, and his hands, also swathed in bandages, rested on his stomach. His brown hair was matted, and perspiration caused by pain glistened on his brow.

Magistrate Wolf approached the settle. "Jacques Monet?"

"Yes," the younger man growled.

"You are under arrest on two counts of attempted murder."

Jacques jutted out his chin defiantly and glared up at the official. "Humph," he snorted angrily, "you've made a mistake. I don't know these people. And I certainly haven't killed anyone." Clenching his teeth on a groan, he turned his head away as he gritted out, "I'm an agent with the Hanseatic League. I live at Number 2, Winkelstrasse—right here in Nuremberg. My horse threw me and ran off yesterday afternoon, forcing me to walk back to town." He flicked a glance toward Nick. "This man is trying to frame me."

Undeterred, Magistrate Wolf instructed the doctor, "He is under house arrest. For no reason are you to release him. When I confirm his address and the existence of a run-away horse, I'll get back to you."

The magistrate turned to leave and then turned back. "Any belongings that might further our investigation?"

"Why, I . . . that is . . .perhaps."

A low growl came from Jacques when Dr. Graber retrieved a battered metal box from a nearby cabinet.

"This fell out from under his tabard when I helped him into the house." He handed the container to the magistrate and made a wry face. "As you can see, I haven't opened it."

Jacques struggled to get up, sending the stack of pillows propped under his legs tumbling to the floor.

The doctor restrained him with a hand on his shoulder. "If you are innocent, young man, you have no cause for alarm. Am I not right?"

Repressing a curse, Jacques sank back on his makeshift bed.

Nick darted one more glance at Jacques, but the patient kept his head down.

When Nick and Magistrate Wolf returned to the sleigh, the official settled on the front seat with the metal box resting on his knees. Although Nick had to watch where he was going, he couldn't resist stealing glances at the magistrate, who determinedly tried to pry open the box with his fingers.

Finally, frustrated with his failed efforts, Magistrate Wolf slapped the box against his knee and bellowed, "Stop at the nearest smithy."

They hadn't gone far before Bert spied a smithy's guild sign—a horseshoe hanging on a pole—down a side street. Pointing to the right, he shouted, "There's a smithy—over there."

Nick jerked hard on the reins and swung the team around the corner so sharply that he barely missed the corner of the building. The sleigh skidded on one runner, screeching as it lurched over the icy, snow-covered cobbles. Magistrate Wolf grabbed frantically at the sleigh rails.

"Whohee!" Bert shouted with glee.

When they'd successfully made the turn, the sleigh bounced back down on both runners.

"That was some driving," Magistrate Wolf commented dryly, settling back on the seat. Bert didn't say a word, but his eyes gleamed with excitement.

When the sleigh halted beside the smithy, Magistrate Wolf leaped out and stomped through the snow toward an open shed. A big man wielding long-armed tongs held a horseshoe in the roaring forge. The acrid smell of hot metal hung in the air.

While they watched, the smithy pulled the shoe out of the fire, placed it on a nearby anvil, slammed it decisively with several hammer blows, and then plunged it into a nearby cauldron of water.

While the water sizzled and spit, the smithy looked up at his visitor. "Ja?"

211

"Magistrate Wolf," he identified himself curtly as he held out the metal container. "Open this box—and be quick about it. Break the lock, if need be."

The smithy set aside the horseshoe and slid the hammer back into its slot on the side of the anvil. His sturdy, blackened fingers clamped around the metal box.

Nick, watching from the sleigh, wondered what the magistrate expected to find in that dented old box. Really, it looked worthless.

Bert, too, watched with open-mouthed interest, as if this was the most thrilling thing that had ever happened in his young life.

The smithy pried at the lid with his calloused fingers, but he quickly gave up. Selecting a metal lever from his nearby workbench, he slid it under the lid's edge and broke the lock. He handed the box to the magistrate.

The official flipped a coin at him, grunted "*Danke*," and nodded his appreciation before he wheeled on one heel and marched back to the sleigh.

"Let's go," he ordered, jumping in.

Consumed with curiosity, Nick stole a glance at the magistrate as he raised the lid, but the box faced away from him and the lid blocked his view. The magistrate fiddled with the box, tipping up one end and then the other, obviously trying to dislodge the contents. Finally, the man turned it over and shook it.

And shook it again.

With a loud, exasperated sigh, he slapped the edge against his knee.

Nick's eyebrows shot up when a black book popped out and plunged to the floor boards, landing in the melted snow from the magistrate's boots.

Magistrate Wolf growled something unintelligible as he tossed the empty metal box on the bench between them and reached down to pick up the book. With a couple of broad strokes he swiped it back and forth across his legs to remove the moisture. When he'd secured the volume, clasp up, between his knees, he saw that the hasp was broken.

As Magistrate Wolf cracked open the leather binding, Nick's seeking eyes fixed on *Journal of Pierre Monet* written in bold script on the presentation page. White-faced and stammering, Nick thrust out his arm and pointed at the page. "That-that's the man who k-killed my grandmother!"

Magistrate Wolf pulled back, raised his brows,

and stared at Nick with a measured glance. "Your grandmother's name?" His tone was flat but the question was laden with unspoken meaning .

Nick's voice shook as he stammered his reply, "L-Lady Rose, Lady Rose Sch-Schmidden."

Magistrate Wolf grunted, dropping his eyes to the book. He began flipping the pages, skimming rapidly through the entries.

With difficulty, Nick restrained his questions.

"Hmm," Magistrate Wolf muttered as he clapped the journal shut.

Nick threw him rapid, sideways glances. He didn't wish to appear too eager for information—the magistrate would talk when he was ready—but he certainly wished the man would be a little more forthcoming. What could he possibly have learned in that short time?

"Take me back to my office," he ordered.

At Bert's direction, Nick drove the team several blocks, turned a corner, and then reined to a stop in front of the magistrate's office.

"Come with me, Lord Branden," Magistrate Wolf commanded tersely over his shoulder as he jumped out of the sleigh.

"Be back fer ya mid-day?" Bert asked.

"Sounds good," Nick said, tossing the reins to Bert, who was already scrambling to the front bench.

Nick leaped down to follow Johann Wolf, then turned to watch Bert drive away, proudly perched in the sleigh's front seat, as if imagining himself such a rig's proud owner. In spite of everything that had happened, Nick couldn't help but grin.

CHAPTER SEVENTEEN

Lord Branden and Nick had been gone a long time. Too long, Lady Branden feared. Something was wrong; she sensed it in her spirit. She spent many hours in the chapel reading from the Book of Hours, praying for her husband's and son's safe return, or singing softly.

By the end of the third week, Lady Branden's concern swelled to near-frantic proportions. Each afternoon, determined to maintain her emotional stability and not succumb to fear, she constrained herself to sit quietly in her low chair in the great room and work on her lace collar. Kitty usually joined her with her own project, and they sat by the fireplace in the great room in silence—almost as if voicing their fears might make them a reality.

Today marked the beginning of the fourth week, and even though she was determined to stay on task,

Lady Branden had found herself staring idly into space several times that afternoon. When approaching footsteps in the corridor caught her attention, she stared at the door, paralyzed by hope and fear; the gait sounded like Nicky's—yet it lacked his usual spring. Her heart fluttered uneasily in her chest and she gripped her lace-making board, instinctively bracing herself for bad news.

When the footsteps reached the doorway, Lady Branden lifted her head. Her heart sank to her toes and she bit her lip to keep from crying out. Her son, his clothing stained and wrinkled, with disheveled hair, bloodshot eyes, and several days' growth of dark beard shadowing his face, stood in the doorway. She stared at him, wide-eyed and motionless.

Nick lifted an unsteady hand and shoved his dark hair back off his forehead.

Concern for her son eclipsed Lady Branden's every other thought. She leaped to her feet, sending her lace and bobbin board clattering to the floor and the bobbins rolling in every direction. But she didn't notice.

As he took a step toward her, she stretched out her arms, crying, "Nicky!"

Rushing to her, he folded her in his arms. "Oh, Mama! " his voice carried tender affection, "I came as quickly as I could."

Her hands tightened around his chest. "And where is your Papa?"

Cradling her closer, he emitted a groan that seemed to come from the bottom of his soul. "Papa is—" he choked. "Oh, Mama, he's dead."

Lady Branden felt the color drain from her face, but she managed to whisper, "Whatever grief God allows, we must face with courage." Yet despite her brave words, the strength went out of her legs; she swayed, clutching Nick's arms for support.

Nick bent over, easing her back into her chair.

Her body started to shake, and the pain that exploded in her head was but a shadow of the pain in her heart. Surely, she thought, it would hurt less to die.

* * *

Intending to join Lady Branden, Kitty came down the back stairs carrying her lace and bobbin board. Her footsteps scuffed on the marble floor as she entered the great room. Then she halted, her limbs refusing to move when she saw Nick bent over his mother. Noting his disheveled appearance and Lady Branden's extreme distress, Kitty's mind shouted questions she tactfully chose not to voice.

When Nick raised his head, their eyes met, hers filled with silent questions and his brimming with grief.

Above his mother's head, he mouthed the words, "Papa is dead."

Kitty felt the room start to spin. Lord Branden had always treated her like a daughter, even when she'd been difficult to handle after her parents died, and she loved him devotedly. She dropped her needlework on the nearby game table and clutched the back of the closest chair to steady herself. Tears gushed from her eyes and ran down her cheeks, but she gulped hard and sucked in a sob, determined not to add to the family's distress.

When she could finally speak, her whisper was strained, "And Jacques?"

Nick's blue eyes flashed with a harsh fierceness she'd never seen in them before. "Arrested. I saw to that."

Concern for this family that she loved superseded Kitty's own shock and sent a surge of new-found strength into her spirit; she quietly took charge, suggesting to Nick, "Order yourself a hot bath and something to eat. By the time you've finished, Lenka and I will have your mother settled and you can come back and sit with her." She moved to the fireplace and pulled vigorously on the bell cord to summon help.

When the maid appeared in the doorway, Kitty enlisted her assistance, and between them, they managed to get Lady Branden on her feet

"It's the shock of it, my lady," Kitty forced the encouraging words through her colorless lips. "We'll have you to your room in no time. That's right . . . one foot, now the other."

When Lady Branden was finally resting in her bed, Kitty sent Lenka to the kitchen to fetch hot bricks wrapped in soft cloths. While she waited for Lenka to return, she massaged Lady Branden's cold hands between her own. When Lenka returned with the bricks, Kitty placed them at Lady Branden's feet, pleased to see that the heat immediately eased Lady Branden's tension; as she relaxed, she fell asleep.

Leaving Lenka to watch over Lady Branden, Kitty hurried down the corridor, crossed the second-floor

Joyce Williams

landing where the north and east wings intersected, and then rushed to Nick's room. She rapped firmly on the door with her knuckles.

"Yes. Who's there?" Nick called.

"It's Kitty."

Brief rustling was followed by footsteps padding across the floor. Dressed in fresh hose and a clean shirt, Nick opened the door.

His eyes dark with sorrow, he looked so vulnerable that Kitty yearned to comfort him. When she put out her fingers and touched his arm in a consoling gesture, Nick closed his free hand over hers, and his ragged question betrayed his anxiety, "Is—is she—all right?"

Compassion filled her eyes as they met his. "I think she will be when she's had some rest. She's hardly eaten or slept for days; she sensed something was wrong."

Nick's somber voice was laced with pain. "I'll check on her when I've finished dressing. Then we'll need to contact Father Andrew and make plans for Papa's service." His shoulders, normally so square and confident, sagged with weariness. He nodded mutely and closed the door.

Sorrow burdened Kitty's spirit like a lead weight, and fresh tears sprang up behind her eyes as she fled down the stairs. Instinctively, she sought refuge in the chapel. At the altar, she fell to her knees, pleading brokenly, "Oh, God, help us." She dropped her head to the railing and wept; the pain she'd seen in Nick's eyes seemed more than she could bear.

When her tears finally subsided, words came to her spirit: *Read from the book.*

With a little nod of assent, Kitty stood and leaned over the rail. Grabbing up the Book of Hours from its resting place on the altar, she hugged it to her chest and sank back to the floor.

Her fingers trembled as she released the clasp, lifted the heavy lid, and opened the book. Retrieving the yellow rose with its faintly sweet scent, she slid it onto the floor beside the folds of her navy wool *cotte.*

As she shifted the book on her lap, the pages scrolled to *Hour Seven.* Without seeing, she stared at the open page. Then gradually, she focused on words that uncannily expressed her heart.

> *God is our refuge and strength, a very present help in trouble. Therefore will not we fear . . .*

The appropriateness of the psalm's message generated new confidence in Kitty's heart. In a burst of faith, she repeated the words back to God, as if reminding herself—and Him—of His promises and appropriating His help in their heartache and loss.

Sober and still, she stared up at the stained glass shepherd. His compassionate stance reminded her of words from a verse Lady Branden often quoted . . . words about a shepherd.

She closed the book and started at the beginning, turning one illuminated parchment page at a time until she came to *Hour Four* with its familiar words:

"The Lord is my shepherd; I shall not want . . ."

As she read and re-read the psalm, clinging to its reassuring message, jewel-hued light radiated through the stained glass, illuminating her copper hair, touching her delicate form, enhancing the room's residual aroma of incense. And the sun's bright rays warmed her body and inexplicably lifted the weight of fear and sorrow from her heart.

A song rose to her lips. Spontaneously, she began to sing.

CHAPTER EIGHTEEN

Nick stared at the closed door, the finality of his
father's death pressing down on his heart like a
millstone. He suddenly felt very alone. When,
unconsciously, he reached up and rubbed his arm
where Kitty's hand had rested only moments before,
a sudden yearning for the comfort she represented
overwhelmed him.

In a burst of impulsive energy, he pulled a rust-
colored wool tabard over his head, poked his arms
through the sleeves, and jerked the garment down
over his shirt and hose. Reaching up with both hands,
he smoothed his palms over his tumbled damp hair
and then grabbed his brown leather boots and
jammed his feet into them.

He wrenched open his door and rushed along the
hallway to Kitty's room. When she didn't answer his
fierce knocking, he dashed to his mother's sitting

room in the north wing. He tapped lightly on the door and then leaned against the wall, mopping his forehead against his sleeve.

Lenka cracked open the door and stuck out her head.

Instantly straightening, Nick darted toward her.

Lenka frowned at him, shook her head, and mouthed the words, "Lady Branden is sleeping, my lord. Best not to disturb her.

"Is Kitty here?" Nick demanded, trying unsuccessfully to keep his voice low.

Lenka shook her head and whispered, "No, my lord she left after settling your mother. She hasn't come back . . ."

Nick didn't wait for her to finish her explanation; he sprinted along the hallway toward the back stairs, flew down the steps, and skidded to a halt in the great room, where his mother's lace board and bobbins lay scattered across the floor and Kitty's lace board sat on the game table.

But no Kitty.

He stood there a moment—to catch his breath, to reconsider where she might have gone. And then it came to him.

Of course.

The chapel.

He raced along the corridor and nearly stumbled in his rush across the broad entrance hall. Pausing at the heavy chapel doors, he composed himself before slipping noiselessly inside.

Indeed, there she was, sitting on the floor down front by the altar rail, completely surrounded by the mounded fabric of her full skirt, like a flower in full bloom. Nick's right hand unconsciously stretched out, reaching for the reassurance of her touch. But before he had time to reconsider his impulsive gesture, Kitty began to sing. The music took him so by surprise that he sank down into the nearest pew.

> *"Gentle Shepherd, comfort, lead me.*
> *Tend me with Thy gracious hand . . ."*

Images of his father exploded in Nick's mind and broke through the emotional numbness he'd forced on himself during the days he'd spent in Nuremberg pursuing justice and the long trip home with his sad cargo, burdened with the devastating news he must deliver to his mother and Kitty. As sorrow swept over him in a wave, his self-control crumbled. His anguish spilled out in wrenching sobs.

Kitty broke off singing and turned in time to see Nick's head drop and his forehead thump against the prie dieu in front of him. She hesitated, considering how best to comfort him, then she bowed her head and began to pray.

When Nick's tortured cries finally subsided, Kitty rose to her feet. As she walked slowly up the aisle toward him, the sun shone through the stained glass window behind her, outlining her figure in a halo of light.

Startled by her approaching footsteps, Nick lifted his head. Silent tears washed his cheeks; it was as though a dam had burst and he couldn't stop the flow.

Watching Kitty float toward him, engulfed in sunlight, reminded him of his first sight of her in the upstairs corridor the day he arrived home from Prague. Without conscious thought, he stood to his feet, his arms reaching hungrily for her.

She went willingly into his embrace, and they clung to each other, warmed by the sunshine and each other's touch.

When Nick finally opened his eyes, his gaze met that of the Shepherd in the window, and in that moment his heartbreak and sorrow gave way to the confidence that God was in control and that his dear father dwelt safely in His eternal care. Yes, he would be deeply missed, but their grief was not without hope.

"Sing it again," Nick requested when they later sat side-by-side in the front pew, his arm resting around her shoulders.

"Sing what again?" Her puzzled voice seem to come from a far distance.

"The song you were singing when I came in. You know—the one about the gentle Shepherd."

Kitty lifted her head off his shoulder and pulled back a bit, eyeing him in confusion. "Uh, I just made that up. I-I don't know if I can remember it." Her face brightened, "I think God gave it to me for just that moment in time."

"Try to remember," he begged. "Please."

When Kitty opened her mouth, the words were there.

"Gentle Shepherd, comfort, lead us.
Tend us with Thy gracious hand.
Gentle Shepherd, guide and keep us.
In Thy presence may we stand."

Nick's arm tightened around Kitty's slender frame and he tipped his head to rest against hers. He cradled her close for a long moment, breathing in her familiar jasmine scent. The warm sunshine and the sense of God's presence soothed their aching hearts and made words unnecessary. As they passed through the "valley of the shadow of death," they felt assured that God had not abandoned them in the darkness of grief.

At last, Kitty broke the silence. "Tell me about your trip." Then she qualified, "That is, if you want to."

"It would be a relief." Nick focused on the Shepherd while he recounted the details of the journey: His father slumping over in the sleigh. Jacques knocking him out. Opening his eyes just as Jacques attacked him with his own knife. Fighting off Jacques. Jacques running away in the snow. The long drive to Nuremburg. The inn where he found lodging and discovered his pouch was missing. Sending young Bert into the snowstorm to secure a coffin.

When he described the hooded men and the thud of the coffin lid that made him determined to bring Jacques to justice, tears streaked down Kitty's face. He squeezed her shoulder, then pulled her against his chest as he shared his realization that he was now Lord Branden.

Kitty relaxed in Nick's arms, her cheek against his chest, her ear attune to his heartbeat.

He mentioned the magistrate, Johann Wolf, told about their visit to Dr. Graber, and described Jacques's physical situation.

Nick felt relieved that Kitty listened to him without interrupting, allowing him to freely unburden his heart. However, when he mentioned the metal box containing the leather-bound journal that had belonged to Pierre Monet, his grandmother's music tutor, she stiffened.

"Really!" she exclaimed, and then added, "Oh, Nick, were you—did you get to read it?"

He nodded. "Johann Wolf and I read it together. Come to find out, Wolf's aunt served as a lady's maid for Lord Myer's wife—and they were guests at the wedding when my grandmother disappeared. Johann has heard his relatives talk about it many times over the years. And the journal explained a lot of details I'd never thought about or just didn't understand—like how Pierre Monet knew about Burg Mosel's secret

231

chamber and the way to access it. Before he came to Burg Mosel, he boarded for over a year with his music patron's family in Vienna, and the grandfather who lived with them had, in his younger years, designed secret rooms and passageways. Pierre spent a lot of time with him and learned his secrets.

"Hmm," Kitty murmured, "and the innocent old man never realized his information could cause such tragedy."

They were both silent for a moment before Kitty asked, "Did you bring the journal with you?"

Nick shook his head. "No. I needed to get home with father's body. When Dr. Graber said he'd likely have to amputate Jacques's right leg due to frostbite, I knew his recovery and the trial would take longer than I could stay, so I left it with Johann as evidence."

He sighed wearily before he determinedly continued in a lighter tone, "I did contact the Hanseatic League—father's copy of our contract was in his pouch. I was relieved when they agreed to honor the agreement Jacques had set up for us, because I firmly believe involving ourselves in trade that promotes the growth of local commerce is vital to our long-term survival."

They held each other, basking in the warmth and the sweet smell of incense, each consumed with private thoughts, content to be together in their sorrow.

At last, Nick whispered, "Thank you for listening. It's a weight off my mind to tell someone. When I finished at the university, I thought I understood the world, but this experience opened my eyes to the magnitude of responsibility accompanying my father's title and position. I always knew he was an extraordinary man, but I see now that I never fully appreciated him. Or my mother. She supported him with such quiet strength and discretion that I never realized how much he relied on her judgment."

Kitty pulled back, lifted her hand to touch Nick's face, and suggested,. "Let's go see her."

CHAPTER NINETEEN

"Miss Kitty! Miss Kitty!" Dagmar's hysterical cries preceded her plump, bobbing figure along the corridor to the great room, her stiff skirts crackling like fat on a fire.

Kitty glanced up from her needlework; she'd determined to continue working on her lace table runner each afternoon even though Lady Branden was not well enough to join her.

"What is it, Dagmar?" she inquired when the plump head housekeeper appeared in the doorway, red-faced, her cap askew.

"There's been a fire, Miss Kitty," the older woman sucked in a whistled breath between her teeth and rubbed a soot-covered hand across her forehead, leaving behind a wide black smudge, "in the servants' quarters."

Kitty dropped her lace board and sprang to her

feet. "Is the fire still burning? Is everyone safe?" She sniffed the air for smoke as she sped toward the door.

Dagmar, scrambling to keep up, quickly reassured her. "Yes, everyone's safe. And Josef put out the fire . . ." she left a second black smudge on her right cheek as she brushed back a nagging tendril of gray hair, "but we need to relocate Lenka. She tripped on her rug and smacked into the bedside table; her burning candle tipped onto the bed and the duvet caught fire." Dagmar wrinkled her nose. "Oh, Miss Kitty, burning feathers stink something fierce!"

Kitty nodded her wry agreement as Dagmar continued between panting breaths, "I would have gone to Lady Branden, but with her sick and all, I came to you."

"Why . . ?" Kitty stopped herself from adding "me" and quickly changed her question, "Is there an empty room in the servants' quarters?"

"Yes. But only one. And it's the smallest. Lenka isn't happy about it; she thinks Nora should give up her room—it's bigger, you know—because Lenka is older than Nora and she's *Lady Branden's* maid."

Kitty clamped her lips between her teeth. Just her luck to have to sort out a domestic problem while

Lady Branden was sick. *God, help me*, she silently entreated divine assistance.

"Lenka will have to make do with the small one until we can get her room cleaned and aired. Nora doesn't have to give up her room; the fire wasn't her fault. And Dagmar, you see to righting Lenka's room as soon as you can." A shrewd expression narrowed her eyes. "Tell her I said Lady Branden would be proud of her for being so cooperative."

Dagmar's gray curls bounced with each bob of her head. "Oh, I will, Miss Kitty, I will. Thank you."

With the logistics sorted out, Kitty's thoughts flashed to the fire. "Lenka and Josef are all right? You're sure?"

"Yes, yes. Josef was in the hallway and heard Lenka's call for help. He went right in, and there she was, slapping at the fire with her nightgown. But you know Josef; he's such a take-charge person. He just picked up the end of the duvet and rolled it in on itself. That put the fire out right quick." She stood a little taller. "And I helped him carry it outside."

"Thank you, Dagmar. I'm sure Josef couldn't have done it without you. And that was quick thinking on his part. Tell, him . . . no, I'll speak to him myself."

Kitty lifted her chin; she knew Lady Branden would deal personally with each person involved in the situation if she were able—so that is what she would do.

* * *

Nick and Kitty sat at the dining table for nearly an hour, attempting to eat their evening meal. But nothing seemed right without Lord and Lady Branden. Nick didn't say a word, and Kitty pushed her food around on her plate. The servants tried to behave normally, but they obviously felt the loss, too.

Nick finally scooted his chair back from the table, rose slowly to his feet, and moved toward the door, dejection in every line of his body. Kitty watched him go with sorrowful eyes; nothing she could say could make their sorrow go away.

At the door, Nick stopped. Straightening his shoulders, he turned back, offering Lord Branden's usual invitation in a choked voice, "How about a game of chess, Kitty?"

"Oh!" Kitty felt her chin quiver, and she hurriedly flicked away the tears that blurred her vision and steadied her lips. "Yes . . ." Immediately, she pushed aside her pewter charger and got up from the table.

As she came close to him, her whisper was barely audible, "Thank you, Nicky. I miss him so much." She swallowed hard and forced a brave smile.

Nick caught her hand and twined his fingers through hers. They walked together down the hall to the great room, drawing strength from the comfort found in sharing their grief.

Fifteen minutes later Nick moved his queen into position, announcing, "Checkmate," with a flicker of triumph in his eyes.

Kitty rolled her eyes in a self-deprecating look that said she knew her mind hadn't been on the game. How could it be? This afternoon she'd assured Nora that she didn't have to give up her room. She'd complimented Josef on his quick thinking. And she could still hardly believe she had actually ordered Lenka to stop fussing. No wonder she couldn't focus on the chess game; tragedy had forced her to stretch in ways she'd never dreamed possible.

* * *

Kitty came down for breakfast later than usual. Her stomach growled as she eagerly ladled porridge into her bowl and added a handful of walnuts and a few dried currants.

She'd only taken three bites when Lenka burst into the dining room. "Oh, Miss Kitty, I'm so glad to find you. I'm so worried."

"Yes? What is it?" Kitty met Lenka's uncharacteristic outburst with a reassuring smile; everyone seemed to be unsettled, trying to find their bearings without their master and mistress. "How can I help you?"

"It's Lady Branden, Miss. She keeps insisting that she wants to get up. But I don't think she should; she's just not—right . . ." Lenka's voice wobbled, upsetting her normally reserved demeanor.

Kitty had to catch herself to keep her mouth from dropping open. Lenka—the protective-of-her-position Lenka—was asking the poor-orphan-girl Kitty for help with her mistress.

"Why, Lenka, what do you want me to do?"

"Please, would you come and talk to her? She'll listen to you."

Help me, God, Kitty flashed up her standard silent prayer and couldn't help the quirk at the corner of her mouth; God seemed determined to stretch her. Again.

"I'll be right up, Lenka." She scooped up her bowl

and stood. "Who is with her now?" she questioned, suddenly worried that Lenka might have left Lady Branden alone.

Lenka cleared her throat, trying to get herself back under control. "Nora's there—just until I get back."

"Good. I'll be right up." Kitty carried her bowl to the sideboard as Lenka hurried out the door.

In the corridor outside Lady Branden's suite, Kitty encountered her maid as she was leaving. "Thank you for helping Lenka, Nora. That was very kind of you." Nora beamed; it was plain to see her mistress's approval made her happy.

Acting from a habit of respect, Kitty tapped on Lady Branden's sitting room door and waited. But when she overheard Lenka begging anxiously, "My lady! My lady, please, wait 'til you talk to Miss Kitty," Kitty pushed open the door and dashed through the sitting room.

Relief flooded Lenka's face when Kitty appeared in the bedchamber doorway. "I'm so glad you're here. You've got to make her listen to reason."

Dear God, help me. Kitty sent another prayer heavenward as she stepped into the room. Instantly, she recalled the psalmist's words, *"I will fear no evil, for Thou art with me."*

"Thank you, Lord," her heart whispered. She was learning to recognize and trust God's voice.

Lady Branden was sitting up in bed with the blankets bunched at her waist. Her dark hair, always so carefully dressed, hung down over one shoulder in a long, messy braid. One bare leg stuck out from under the covers and her slender foot dangled toward the floor. Her wide, beautiful eyes stared out vacantly above the unnatural flush that burned her cheeks.

Kitty drew in a deep breath and squared her shoulders. Then she turned to the maid and instructed in her firmest tone, "Lenka, go ask Zina in the kitchen for a muslin bag filled with ice chips from the icehouse. I'll stay with Lady Branden until you return."

When Lenka had departed, Kitty moved slowly toward the bed. In a soothing, sing-song voice, she spoke softly as she touched Lady Branden's shoulder. "How are you feeling today?"

"I'm so hot," Lady Branden fretted plaintively, plucking spasmodically at the duvet.

"Yes, I can see that," Kitty assured her gently, "but I've sent Lenka to fetch a bag of ice chips to help you feel cooler."

Kitty reached behind Lady Branden, retrieved her flattened feather pillow, and pummeled it lightly with her fist, releasing the lavender scent. As she placed the fluffed pillow back against the head of the bed, she noted the pitcher and goblet on the side table. Grasping the pitcher by the handle, she turned and held it up. "Would you like a drink?"

"Yes, please. That would be nice." Kitty pressed her lips together and bit down hard; Lady Branden's weak, wavering voice made her want to cry.

"Good. Let's tuck your foot back under the covers, and then you may have a drink." She bent down and lifted Lady Branden's leg, gently easing it back under the covers. When it rested beside its mate, Kitty picked up the top corners of the duvet and lightly shook it, releasing its soothing scent before she smoothed it back into place.

In a low voice she quoted the words from the psalm, *"The Lord is my Shepherd, I shall not want. He maketh me to lie down . . ."* As she took Lady Branden by the shoulders and gently pressed her back against the pillow, Kitty continued in her sing-song voice, *"in green pastures."*

Relieved to see that the older woman relaxed against the pillow, Kitty filled a goblet and held it to her lips. *"He leads me beside the still waters,"* she whispered. Then, as Lady Branden reached for the goblet, Kitty's words became a prayer, *"He restoreth my soul."*

Lady Branden took a small sip before suddenly shoving the goblet away from her face. Taken by surprise, Kitty tightened her fingers around the stem to prevent the contents from spilling and quickly set the goblet on the side table.

When she turned back, Lady Branden's head had dropped back against the fluffed pillow and her eyes were closed. A second look assured Kitty the older woman was asleep. Overcome with relief, Kitty sank on the nearby chair and whispered the next line of the psalm, *"Yea, though I walk through the valley of the shadow of death, I will fear no evil, for Thou art with me."*

A few minutes later, Kitty heard Lenka enter the sitting room. She tiptoed from Lady Branden's bedside to join the maid in the outer room. Reaching for the bag filled with ice chips, Kitty whispered her thanks and gestured for the maid to follow her.

Lenka took one look at her mistress and froze in place. Her strained face turned white. "Oh, Miss Kitty! Is she . . . ?" Her mouth twitched and her eyes suddenly gushed tears.

Kitty shook her head, her lips framing the words, "No, just sleeping."

As she observed the maid, Kitty suddenly sensed that keeping Lenka busy would be the best thing for her. "Lift the bottom of the duvet," she whispered. "I'm going to wrap this cold bag in her hand towel and put it against her feet."

Like a coil unwinding, Lenka sprang into action. She lifted the duvet and held it up while Kitty propped the towel-covered bag of ice against Lady Branden's feet. With a nod to Lenka to release the duvet, Kitty straightened up. As she did, she noticed the dark circles under the maid's eyes and the weariness in her face. Gesturing toward the sitting room, Kitty led the way out of the bed chamber.

"Lenka, were you here all night?"

"Yes, Miss," Lenka replied. "I couldn't leave her— so restless and all."

"That was an excellent decision, Lenka, but now it's my turn. I'll stay with Lady Branden this morning while you get some rest; come back after lunch." She waved the maid toward the door.

"Oh, thank you, Miss Kitty!" Obviously embarrassed by her overt display of emotion, Lenka scurried out of the room.

Kitty pursed her lips, raised her brows, and looked up—as if questioning God. It kept happening: everyone did precisely what she told them to do.

* * *

"Father Andrew is coming tomorrow," Nick announced, at the end of another dinner eaten in silence. "He'll need to stay overnight. Will you see to it?"

Kitty's eyes flew to Nick's. She'd hardly seen him for the past several days; she knew he was paying visits to the villages on the estate in an effort to reassure everyone that he would follow in his father's footsteps. She'd forgotten all about the Vigil service tomorrow night and the funeral the next morning. Oh, how could she have been so thoughtless?

"What time should we expect him to arrive?"

"Late afternoon, I should think," Nick replied.

Kitty stared blindly at the candelabra illuminating the table. "I'll tell cook to plan on including him tomorrow night for dinner. And ask her to prepare a couple of smoked pheasants for our mid-day meal after the internment."

When she finally brought her gaze back to Nick, she started strong, "Your mother isn't well enough to be up yet. She'll be so sad . . ." her voice cracked before she continued in a whisper, "when she realizes what she missed."

They both stared at their food.

Finally Nick broke the silence. "They had a good life together. He was a good husband. He was a good master. He was a good fath . . ." He ducked his head, scraping the chair legs across the floor as he jumped up and fled from the room.

What do I do now? Kitty wondered, staring after him. Nick had accepted comfort from her once before . . . Should she go to him?

She didn't have to look for him or wonder where he'd gone; she heard the harpsichord before she reached the dining room door. As she headed toward the great room, the walls echoed with the force of his playing.

The servants had built a fire in the great room fireplace and its leaping shadows writhed eerily on the mahogany paneled walls. The heavy curtains that enclosed the music room hung slightly apart, just enough so she could see that Nick was playing in the dark. Did that mean he wanted to be alone with his music, with his grief?

Curling her feet under her, Kitty settled in Lord Branden's oversized chair that was still pulled up near the fireplace—where he'd last sat in it. How long ago that seemed. Yet, sometimes she caught herself listening for his footsteps in the corridor, her mind forgetting—or denying—his death.

The loud, unharmonious crash of harpsichord keys interrupted Kitty's musing, propelling her out of the chair and across the room. As she pushed aside the curtain, her heart skipped a beat. Nick's shoulders were slumped and his forehead rested on his arms crossed on the instrument. Her heart ached for his loss. She scooted onto the bench next to him without speaking; she felt so helpless, knowing nothing she could say could change the situation.

Nick turned and wrapped his arms around her and buried his head against her neck. She could feel his shoulders shaking with his sorrow. When he finally released her, he choked out, "S-Sometimes I can't get the pictures out of my mind. He was so alive one minute and the next—" he gasped in a harsh cry, "h-he was dead on the floor of the sleigh. Oh, Kitty, I had to close his eyes." He gritted his teeth before continuing. "I keep hearing the casket lid crash— crash shut." He wiped his hand over his eyes and down his face, as if to scrub away the memory. "I h-hear it in my sleep, and I wake up with a start— covered in sweat."

He pulled away from her, trembling with emotion, mumbling, "So sorry to go over all this again."

Kitty felt her own grief rise up to mingle with his; it squeezed her chest and strangled her throat. Tears ran down her cheeks and dripped off her chin. She clung to Nick's arm and leaned her head against his shoulder. She knew that even with God's comfort, the loss would be felt for a long time. Suppressing or denying their grief would only prolong the sadness and the adjustment.

Softly, she began to whisper the psalmist's words, *"The Lord is my Shepherd . . ."*

CHAPTER TWENTY

Cocooned in warm blankets, Lady Branden peered over them from her place of rest in her favorite chair in her sitting room. It was her first day up since she'd been put to bed more than a fortnight ago.

"Is there anything else I can get for you?" Kitty inquired solicitously; she would willingly do anything to express the overflowing thanksgiving she felt toward God for sparing this woman who'd been her mother's friend and who'd taken her in as an orphaned child and loved her so unconditionally.

Lifting her eyes to Kitty's sweet face, Lady Branden whispered, "A drink, please." She hesitated before adding, "And would you read to me from the Book of Hours?"

Nick, who'd been staring moodily at the fire in the fireplace, turned around as Kitty exclaimed, "Oh, that's just what we all need."

"I'll get it," he volunteered, disappearing out the door with a hint of his old bounce in his steps. Hearing his hurrying footsteps, the two women exchanged a glance of shared affection.

Kitty lifted the pitcher from the dressing table, poured a drink for Lady Branden, and waited while she sipped it.

"Thank you, my dear. For everything," Lady Branden whispered, returning the goblet.

Kitty sat down on the chaise, leaned back and closed her eyes, waiting for Nick. The passing of time didn't seem to matter anymore; Nick was safely home and Lady Branden would recover.

When Nick returned, cradling the heavy book in the crook of his arm, he dropped to the chaise beside her. Kitty sat up and reached out to take the book. But Nick shook his head. "No, let me read to you."

He unfastened the clasp, handed the delicate rose to Kitty for safekeeping. and then proceeded to flip through the pages. He paused several times before settling on *Hour Nineteen*.

He read aloud:

I love the Lord, because he hath heard
My voice and my supplications.

Because he hath inclined his ear unto me,
Therefore will I call upon him as long as I live.
The sorrows of death compassed me,
And the pains of hell gat hold upon me:
I found trouble and sorrow.

When Nick's voice roughened, Kitty slipped her hand around his arm and pressed her cheek to his shoulder. Lady Branden bowed her head and closed her eyes. Tears seeped from beneath her dark lashes and slid down her pale cheeks.

Return unto thy rest, O my soul;
For the Lord hath dealt bountifully with thee.
For thou hast delivered my soul from death,
Mine eyes from tears, and my feet from falling.
I will walk before the Lord in the land of the living.

Clearing his throat, Nick finished strong.

What shall I render unto the Lord for all his
benefits toward me?
I will take the cup of salvation, and call upon
the name of the Lord.
I will pay my vows unto the Lord now in the
presence of all his people.
Precious in the sight of the Lord is the death
of his saints.
O Lord, truly I am thy servant . . .

Nick slowly closed the book and lifted his head. His eyes burned and conviction firmed his voice. "I've always believed what I was taught, but now the scriptures seem—relevant. And God seems real."

Too moved for words, Kitty hugged his arm supportively.

Lady Branden's chest rose and fell with a long breath. Then she smiled tremulously and whispered, "You are very wise to consider the spiritual foundation of your life. Without God, the disappointments, heartaches, and loneliness are too difficult to bear . . ." Tears choked her voice.

Nick crossed the room and dropped to his knees beside his mother. He rested his head against her knee.

Kitty followed, kneeling on the other side.

Lady Branden caressed her son's cheek and smoothed his dark hair. Then she reached a hand out to each of them and brought their hands together on her lap. "You are both so dear to me." Her tremulous smile, full of hope, was like sunshine after the rain. "I know we can never go back . . . but we can go forward."

Nick lifted his head, and his eyes rested on

Kitty's bowed head. He squeezed her hand and when she lifted her chin, he smiled, raising his brows in an invitation.

Kitty stared back at Nick. Did she dare respond to the love she saw in his eyes? Did she dare to face him as an equal? She found she couldn't help herself—her tremulous lips returned his smile as Lady Branden patted their clasped hands, her gaze warm with affection.

After they said goodnight to Lady Branden and left her in Lenka's care, Nick carried the Book of Hours back to the chapel. Walking beside him, Kitty silently reflected that God had been gracious, and her heart rejoiced in spite of her sadness. Who would ever have believed that good could come out of their heartache?

But it had.

Kitty pushed open the chapel door and held it for Nick, then followed him inside.

Pausing in the aisle to look up, Nick bent one knee and nodded his head, acknowledging the presence of Christ the Shepherd before he moved to the front. When the precious book was back in its place on the altar, he turned to Kitty, who had moved to stand beside him. Extending his hands and catching hers, he blurted impulsively, "Kitty, you're— different somehow."

Kitty studied their intertwined hands as she struggled to find the words to express her heart. Nick had to bend near to hear her whisper, "God has brought good out of our sorrow. When Lady Branden first became ill, the servants came to me for directions. I was terribly afraid, but I knew God was challenging me to trust Him."

She lifted her face and fixed her gaze on the Shepherd. "He gave me courage, and He inspired me to advise them to do what I knew Lady Branden would have told them. In turn, He showed me that they respect me—and that I am a capable and valuable person, regardless of my station at birth."

Nick squeezed her fingers reassuringly, but he opened and closed his mouth twice before he finally whispered, "Does this mean—Oh, Kitty, are you ready to accept my love?"

In that moment, the wall of fear Kitty had held between them crumbled. As their eyes met, she slowly nodded her bright head.

"I don't know the future, Kitty, but I promise I

will always love you." Nick's blue eyes burned into hers. "Will you be my wife?"

Kitty studied Nick's face. Fire and suffering had tried his soul. A new maturity emanated from within him. And God had indeed healed her heart and erased her feelings of inadequacy. She had saved Nick's life, and she could now stand beside him as an equal before God—and man.

"Yes, my lord," she replied simply.

The significance of those two words, rejected by Kitty so many years ago, struck Nick with visible force; he sucked in a sharp breath as his eyes filled with tenderness. The honor he'd so foolishly demanded of her in his youth was now freely given. Humbled by her sweet reverence, Nick exclaimed, "Oh, that God would make me worthy."

Under the smiling Shepherd, the dark head bent to the bright one as they sealed their pledge to each other and to God with a lovers' kiss.

Made in the USA
Charleston, SC
29 November 2014